PRAISE FOR *DAPHNIS AND CHLOE*

"A classic tale rung through the contemporary ringer, narrated by the one and only LOVE, that universal townie that's always hovering in the corner when the party turns sour. Is LOVE at fault, at play, the saver of the everloving day, or, as per usual, the party ouroboros? Do they 'conquer all' or just snag a case of beer and que sera out the back door? Step inside, grab a Solo cup and see."

—IAN McCORD, REC ROOM BOOKS (ATHENS, GA)

"A dark fable underlined by a glowing current, this slim novel is an incantation, a reminder of the human story we all already know in our bones. Sketched anew in stark contrast against the ocean, the land, and the car mechanic shop, this is a story of parentage, destined lovers, brutal bikers, and the underbelly of a city. Doesn't daylight show us the contours of darkness itself, asks McAdam? In the words of the author: 'It might not look like love, but it was.' Anyone with a romantic bone in their body will be enchanted by McAdam's prose and the way this dark story will slide into your heart: sturdy, reliable, true in the old way."

—JULIA PAGANELLI MARIN,

PEARL'S BOOKS (FAYETTEVILLE, AR)

"This short, but powerful novel draws you in with the sense of a modern myth. In a fresh way, it tells of the ache of love and heartbreak; desire and longing, innocence and darkness; and predators and prey. I was completely drawn into this story."

—KATRINA BRIGHT-YERGES,
BOOKS & COMPANY (OCONOMOWOC, WI)

"A gorgeously written, unsettling retelling of an old story. It packs a lot in so few pages but it stays with you long after you're done."

—MATT BURRIS, MAGIC CITY BOOKS (TULSA, OK)

"This dark modern reimagining of the ancient story of two foundlings whose love—at first innocent, then lost, ultimately to be found again—is told by Eros himself. Despite the horrific circumstances that separate them, and the violence that ensues, they learn with love, there is hope. A small volume that packs a powerful punch. A propulsive, mesmerizing read."

—ALANA HALEY, SCHULER BOOKS (GRAND RAPIDS, MI)

PRAISE FOR COLIN McADAM

"His voice is original and fiercely intelligent. It somehow possesses this combination of hard-won world weariness and exuberant, unshakeable faith in a better world. The essence of his prose, for me, is contradiction . . . my favourite thing . . . contradictions and layers and layers of meaning. He exposes all of our treacherous and base instincts but with the unspoken caveat that, in spite of our horrible human ways, we must always, relentlessly, struggle to love each other."

—MIRIAM TOEWS, AUTHOR OF *A COMPLICATED KINDNESS*

"McAdam teases and turns around language, giving us a creative and wondrous portrait of nonhuman society from the inside out."

—DAN KOIS, *SLATE*

"Both disarmingly familiar and richly, movingly strange."

—SAM SACKS, *WALL STREET JOURNAL*

DAPHNIS AND CHLOE

COLIN McADAM

BIBLIOASIS
WINDSOR, ONTARIO

FIRST EDITION
10 9 8 7 6 5 4 3 2 1

Library and Archives Canada Cataloguing in Publication
Title: Daphnis and Chloe / Colin McAdam.
Names: McAdam, Colin, author.
Identifiers: Canadiana (print) 20260168688 | Canadiana (ebook) 2026016884X
ISBN 9781771967235 (softcover) | ISBN 9781771967242 (EPUB)
Subjects: LCGFT: Novels.
Classification: LCC PS8575.A26 D37 2026 | DDC C813/.6—dc23

Edited by Daniel Wells
Copyedited by John Sweet
Cover and text designed by Ingrid Paulson
Cover image of Cupid: Hans Makart (Austrian, 1840–1884), *A Ceiling Painting, Society Lady With Cupid In A Garden Landscape*, c. 1877.

Canada Council for the Arts | Conseil des Arts du Canada
Ontario Arts Council | Conseil des arts de l'Ontario
Ontario
Canada
Ontario Creates | Ontario Créatif

Published with the generous assistance of the Canada Council for the Arts, which last year invested $153 million to bring the arts to Canadians throughout the country, and the financial support of the Government of Canada. Biblioasis also acknowledges the support of the Ontario Arts Council (OAC), an agency of the Government of Ontario, which last year funded 1,709 individual artists and 1,078 organizations in 204 communities across Ontario, for a total of $52.1 million, and the contribution of the Government of Ontario through the Ontario Book Publishing Tax Credit and Ontario Creates.

PRINTED AND BOUND IN CANADA

For my brother, Sean

And in memory of Max Eisen,
Friend and great survivor

PROLOGUE

One of my favourite stories begins with a prayer that it will bring pleasure to many and comfort to the sad, and it was written by its author to refresh the memory of those who have been in love. No one, he says, has ever escaped the attack of Love and no one ever will as long as there is beauty and eyes to see it.

I work in a place for people near the end of their lives, where the beauty isn't obvious, where some can no longer see. I set up games for them, organize their days, and best of all I tell them stories.

Most of these people are old, although some have come early to the end of their abilities. I myself, strangely, am older than all of them, but somehow I stay fairly rooted in summer. I can't stop loving surprises.

People live here for years sometimes, others come soon after having a fall or a stroke and last no more than a day.

I don't think of it as a place where people die, I think of it as a home for their final visions; whatever hope, mischief, love, and sadness remain to play out. Anger, too. A day won't go by without someone screaming at a ghost, a child who betrayed her. Old men shouting at their bodies that will no longer do their bidding.

The best part of my job is learning about their lives. Ask yourself to picture a hero and you likely won't see one of these hunched and shuffling characters, drooling old women with walkers, but these people are my heroes. I know what all of them have been through.

I sit with them at tables and listen.

Some remember very little and some can't even speak, but a mute old man cutting pictures out of a magazine can tell me much about what he was or hoped to be. His scissors finding photos of trees and furniture, grandkids and women with brown hair.

Most of them remember reading. These letters, for whatever reason, are some of the only things they recall. And books can be a great comfort to them.

Among my tasks, I manage the little library over there at the back of the recreation room.

For over a year now I have come to know a certain couple. He is blind and she can no longer speak from a stroke. She can read but not out loud and he, of course, needs to be read to if he wants to learn a story.

They came to this place together and share a room. Husbands and wives will sometimes arrive here and forget each other, but these two seem to walk in the same skin. They help each other get dressed. She combs his remaining hair and pushes his wheelchair, she having learned to walk again and he unable on feet enfeebled from burns.

I don't exactly read to them. I like to think that I am inspired by their stories and breathe them back into their days, their memories, just as my fellow god Ares might make a disheartened warrior brave in battle by whispering strong words.

The blind man has told me about some of their life, the business they had. He complains about taxes and insurance companies and the array of strangers who directed the movement of his hands and tongue, the array so vast and baffling that his growing dementia is no doubt attributable to the world being too entangled.

Holding his wife's hand one day, he said to me, "This, you see, makes sense."

And I know it.

I know it.

A long time ago a poet asserted that Love was the fourth of the gods to appear, before the universe became whole.

Chaos was first, then Earth, then Hell.

Only after the emergence of Love did things like Time and Space come about, because Love brings mischief and mystery.

The poet said it wasn't until Night fell in love that Daylight first appeared, and of course once light was available and the gods could see lines and curves more clearly... well, we have thunder and oceans and eyes.

If I told you how long I have lived, you wouldn't believe me. And if I said I am Love, you would wonder why I work here. There are more attractive jobs to have, those that don't trade in tragedies and bedpans. That woman over there who hasn't moved on her own in weeks—I know she will die tomorrow. And that man who moans with an open mouth while his friends hit a green balloon around the room... Surely Love should attend to the young, to the future.

We have a greenhouse here, and a chapel. A large space for line dancing and lawns for when the weather is good.

And this niche over here where the water fountain is—I made that golden mosaic.

I learn everyone's story, you see. Either the things they have done in my name or the bitterness they endured without me. And I try to make things with what I learn from them.

Art provides the order and simplicity to me that the blind man gets from holding his wife's hand. The same combination of understanding and wonder. I have seen so many murderers and depressives and others having naked lunches in the sun, squeezing lemon over their tongues, and I wonder how to attach this world to a sentence like a butterfly on a pin.

Not long ago the mute woman stared at my mosaic as she stood behind her husband in his wheelchair. She was moved by the scenes depicted—I could tell—and she came around beside her husband to get closer. She wanted to tell him what she saw.

"It's an old story," I said to them. "First told two thousand years ago, in a different form, about a couple named Daphnis and Chloe."

My mosaic contained a sky of gold that arched and curved over the top of the niche. There were scenes of women giving birth, of strangers dressing the babies, the babies being left and raised by others.

Above the fountain was a depiction of young people pledging love as enemies gathered around them. Men and women wept and died, and a battle took place between all manner of predators and prey. Over here was a young woman crying, and beneath that a terrible fire.

There were too many bodies unmourned.

A darkness at the edge of every square made the brightness rich and deep, and the couple at the centre were involved in most of the scenes—often watched over by a dog with black ears.

I put a hand behind her back, gently, and suggested we walk towards their room.

"Do you want me to tell you the story?" I asked them.

The man was saying something and I leaned over to hear him better.

"I knew a bad man once," he said.

BOOK ONE

2

There's a city on an island in the Pacific that you reach by ferry from the mainland. A city given shade by giant cedars with a past as dark as the eye of its creator, who stood on a hill, let's say, more than a million years ago and looked down and declared *this will be*. Eye dark as oil, mischief flickering in it from the flame of an ancient lamp.

The city had landlords and rich retired women. Downtown streets, a wooded coast, and a place to get tattoos. The island around it was vast, bigger than many countries, its woods so deep that there may yet have been creatures within not seen by human eyes, in this world where many are convinced there cannot, ever more, be wonders.

Sleeping wildcats drooped over branches like ribbons and on the beaches wolves ate deer.

In the shopping mall teens fell in love and fought, and some, though they never said it, wanted to be at home with their parents, to draw, to sing, to feel honest.

A mechanic named Frank owned a garage with his old friend Charlie.

Many years ago they had met on a bus, both of them immigrants from Greece, and their lives had taken strangely parallel paths thereafter. They both chose names that appeared less Greek, they opened the garage together, both marrying women they adored with whom they could have no children.

The couples went on trips together, laughing and fighting, sometimes entertaining an exchange of partners, but only saying so in whispers to each betrothed, only saying so as fellow yearners who saw the sun of life, still warm, subsiding towards the horizon.

On the upper coast, once, they had rooms in a nice hotel. They went on a hike together in the forest, dark and damp. And with Frank in the lead, a black bear rose from the place where Death comes and charged at him. Charlie and the women shouted, hiding behind each other, and Frank, as he told it, simply held still, understanding.

The bear was protecting her cubs.

She was Time, embodied, a force unstoppable saying I am the past, my children are the future, and this, the present, will be conquered.

Frank understood it all, in that moment, and he bowed to it. He dared not look the bear in the eyes and he said to his wife and friends, "Back up." He knew to be neither proud nor scared.

He touched Lina's face that night and saw their past, wondered where they were going. "I could smell berries on her breath. The bear's," he said.

At the garage, he and Charlie no longer cursed when their wrenches slipped, when they burned their hardened fingers. They had more than enough business and liked to listen to the stories of their clients, though one day did look a lot like another.

There were drugs on the streets of that city that took away pain for strings of minutes and brought synthetic rapture. People, young and old, who felt that rapture, let their bodies lead them in a dance and the dance went on through the night, with strangers, and they danced on their backs and knees. Children were born from the drugs and the dance had no room for children, and every now and then a baby was left on the sidewalk.

Frank was driving to the pharmacy one night and he parked right next to that path where a mother's journey ended. Rain had fallen, like it did most days, and the sidewalk made a wet bed for a boy wearing nothing but a blanket.

Next to the baby was a bone-handled knife and a locket on a chain.

There were people around to reach or cry out to, police could be summoned with effort. But Frank didn't think to do any of that. Perhaps it was the same calm he felt when the bear came charging at him. *If he's here when I come back,* he said to himself, *I'll take him.*

Frank went into the pharmacy, forgetting what he had come for. He bought a box of diapers and came back out to the sidewalk where the baby remained wet but silent.

Lina looked at the knife and the locket and the baby. She wrapped the knife and locket in a cloth which she kept in the cupboard with her mother's china, and after shaking with nerves and staring and calming his cries, they realized that whenever they held that boy's little body, the world seemed to warm and swell. The sun delayed its journey.

They called him Daphnis, the name of a childhood friend of Frank's who, as far as Frank knew, was the only blond boy in Greece.

And two years went by.

At the garage they kept a lockbox outside the front door where people could leave their keys. A light-blue van was left in the laneway and in the lockbox were its key and also a note.

TAKE EVERYTHING, it said.

Charlie was the first one there that morning.

Frank was often late because of the baby, and Charlie had been picking up the slack. Maybe a little edgy or itchy was Charlie, though he never begrudged the new colour he saw in Frank's face, and he was uncle to the new little boy.

Charlie opened up the van and it was hung with photos of naked women. All of them in black and white, women of various ages, some with bruises and smiling eyes. Beautiful, no doubt, and each in a different circumstance might have conjured a song. But there they hung like indecent trophies, the indecency not in the figures themselves but in the eye of whoever took the pictures.

And there on a bed in the back of the van, lying still on a faux fur blanket, was a baby.

Another one. A girl, although Charlie didn't know that right away.

She didn't move and, like the van, was light blue, and Charlie said, "No, no, no," while he held her.

So many uncomfortable things had Charlie turned away from, those first forty years of his life. Ashamed of his fears and ashamed of the things he sought, this van with the smiles and bruises seemed to bring them all together.

The girl was alive, he realized.

She responded to his warmth. He hugged her and rocked her and sat on the bed, and it seemed that the reason she had been light blue was that she had been stifling a cry.

A terrifying cry, which grew in range and pitch until the girl was red not blue, and the cry seemed to go through seasons, maturing, until it became, for years ahead, the richest and most honest declaration the girl could make of how unspeakably she loved the man who held her.

Like Frank, Charlie's first thought was not to call the police.

Next to the girl on the bed had been left a gold belt, a pair of gold high heels with red soles that seemed incongruously expensive, and a thin gold bracelet or anklet, with a bangle: the letter *C*.

Charlie took the photos down while he held the girl in one arm. He rested her on his belly while he eased the van from the laneway into the shop.

That morning, his wife started looking for baby names beginning with that letter and they both agreed on Chloe.

Frank, Charlie, Lina, and Sue spent the next many years raising those babies as their own. The women learned from each other as mothers; and each felt her child was a miracle. Both kids abandoned, with inscrutable beginnings, both mothers felt, perhaps, a greater need to keep life's hazards away. They hoped for perpetual safety and innocence, yet both women, also, had lived full lives and knew at some level that it was not their birthright to be safe but to be scared. They wanted their kids to be brave.

Lina let Daphnis cry himself to sleep, and Sue tried the same with Chloe but sometimes ended up crying more than the girl. For years the mothers spent every day together. They didn't have a lot of money to go to zoos and movies, so they made their own fun on foggy beaches or at the daycare free on Wednesdays. "Let's get on with it" and "Have fun today" were phrases heard often in those houses, Lina's strong thumbs wiping food and dirt from both kids' faces and each woman trying to shun the world of purse-lipped finger-waggers telling mothers to be perfect.

The families lived a block apart in a neighbourhood where every house had thirty feet to present a front to the world. Salespeople, plumbers, and nurses, everyone hoping to get a little more money or luck and some suspecting that they might not. Lots of new marriages and every now and then a fight that neighbours heard or heard about.

Nothing on that island was far from mountains or forests, but it sometimes seemed that the real wilderness was within each house. Divorces, children lost to drunk drivers, and mothers lost to drink. The four adults watched neighbours come and go.

Daphnis and Chloe played together from the beginning. They walked and then rode bikes to each other's house and to a nearby park that grew from an Eden to a Camelot over the years. Both liked to make things with their hands and to tell each other stories. They chased and held crickets, Chloe wished she could fly with the eagles, and Daphnis once found a carpenter's marking knife that he used to carve shapes in branches and wood: a snake, a car, and a pirate ship.

They had separate friends at school, but they always met in the afternoons and played or hung out until dinner. Riding their bikes in the woods and around the neighbourhood streets, sweaty and thrilled and full of a need to seek and play, and to love.

They grew up quickly.

So lovely at every stage, spreading a calm and charm with their manner and their beauty. In another age they would have been considered high-born. But despite their popularity among kids and adults, they seemed to find the greatest pleasure, the richest simplicity, in being alone with each other.

In the woods one day, Daphnis climbed a tree and slipped, falling backwards and breaking his arm at the elbow. Chloe walked both bikes home beside him. She gave him double-rides for the rest of the summer and he didn't want to go back to school with a cast, so he cracked it himself on his driveway with a stone, while she laughed and said, "You're an idiot."

I have known many people, most of them old, who look at a moment in their life, a glance, a smile, and lose their breath at the sweetness of it. A wink of light reminding them that they won't be here long, a glimpse of the fact that a rich man doesn't know the magic of an apple like the man who owns nothing else. The harder their lives get, the more these moments become unbearably sweet.

Perhaps because they were older when those babies came into their lives, Sue and Lina knew many of those glimpses.

Muted light of the Pacific Northwest on an ocean calm and chilly. They left Chloe's stroller in the car and carried her squirming to the beach while Daphnis ran ahead.

Burrowing clams threw little arches of water from the sand that the kids loved to chase. Trying to predict where each spurt would come from and running towards the holes.

There were other families on the beach, kids for them to race against. Daphnis was fast to the spouts of water and Chloe tended to linger, sitting down and trying to find or get a hold of the clams that retreated under the sand.

Another boy ran with Daphnis, not as fast, who cried whenever he was beaten to the spouts.

I brought a silver light that day. Sent it off the ocean and across the mothers' eyes, off the eyes of Chloe and a dog who shook and sprayed her with sea water while those gleeful little arches jumped around the beach and made it look like the sand was leaking upwards. Sue felt compelled to say, "Who knows." Thinking of her own mother who came and went through her life, not knowing what destiny these kids were carrying in their blood.

"My mom used to say, 'If you work hard...' You know? All that shit. And remember, this was a woman who sat around drinking and left us when she ran out of money. She said, 'If you work hard, you can have what you want,' and then one day you could tell she was just tired of lying. She said, 'It doesn't matter what you do. You've gotta find the right people. That's all'."

Sue held Lina's hand.

"I guess that's why she left."

She laughed as she said it and made Lina smile.

Lina looked around at the kids and said, "Do you wonder who they'll be?"

She wanted Daphnis to beat the other kid to the clams.

"Who knows," said Sue.

The other boy stopped running entirely now and cried louder. Daphnis went over to him and put his arm around his shoulder.

Sue saw the light I'd brought. Warmer. Seeing her friend's bright eyes, Daphnis comforting the boy, Chloe elbow-deep in the sand and laughing at who knows what. Her heart skipped for a moment.

"I mean, if this is what we get out of life, it's enough," she said.

The families spent so much time together that they often had similar thoughts.

One night Charlie and Frank even had the same dream.

At that point Daphnis was fifteen and Chloe two years younger. Business at the garage was steady.

The dream, as each told the other, involved a handsome young man who seemed to Frank and Charlie to be arrogant. A way about him that drew people to him, charming but repulsive at the same time.

In the dream, Daphnis and Chloe were sleeping in the bunk bed at Charlie's. The young man came into the room and woke the boy and girl up. Before he sat on the lower bunk, he touched the foreheads of the children as if to prepare them for a thought.

"You should stay in the garage and work for each other's father," he said.

"Strange," said Charlie, and Frank said the same.

"Why should they stay at the garage?" said Charlie, and Frank asked, "How can we have the same dream?"

They had saved for several years, those families. They might have renovated their kitchens or taken holidays in the winter. At one point the four parents said to each other what the couples had privately been thinking. There was something about those things the babies had been left with, the shoes, the locket, something about that knife with the handle of bone. Lina had unwrapped that knife from the cloth sometimes and thought it must be expensive. The weight of it, the quality of the steel. She had thought about getting it appraised but then worried that someone might recognize it and take away her son.

And Charlie had looked into those high heels. That red sole was distinctive and meant they were a pricey brand. He saw similar shoes listed for thousands of dollars.

Despite where they had found the babies and what they had seen of this unpredictable world, both pairs of parents believed not only that they had come from some special place but that they were destined for something great.

And that was not Frank and Charlie's garage.

For weeks each man asked the other, "What did you dream about last night?" And if they could remember or were not too embarrassed, they revealed their visions and they were never the same again. In fact, a few times Frank said to Charlie, "You might want to talk to someone."

Many events in the history of the world have been built on dreams or less. For now they decided there was no harm in adding a trade to their children's gathering charms. Frank apprenticed Chloe, and Daphnis learned from his uncle Charlie.

The men met customers at the office in the front and were careful not to reveal that the cars were sometimes being worked on by two kids.

After school they met in the garage and learned about gears and grease, about brakes, wiring, air intake, and all the sacred properties of combustion, that force that took us from dwelling on the ground to flying above our troubles.

What magic! That a spark can bring our parents home so quickly, a series of invisible explosions can drive billions of souls, right now, quickly towards the things they want, the people they love, away from the things they fear.

Daphnis and Chloe took to the work immediately. They felt important learning these mysteries, and a sense of responsibility. There was something about the atmosphere of that garage, always warm, the radio on, the older mechanics joking. For Chloe, somewhere in her body were memories of being saved here.

Charlie had kept that van for her, painting it red and keeping it in good shape. It was a place where he himself had learned to be comfortable with his fear—questions about someone leaving a baby in a van full of dirty pictures—Charlie learning to be inside the dark places and bring his own light. He put a new bed in there for Chloe and it became a refuge for her, a bedroom away from her own at the house, and she decorated it, making clouds from cushion stuffing which she hung from the roof with tape and string and putting her drawings and paintings on the walls. The van was always parked in a corner of the garage and they all respected it as Chloe's.

Sue drove her to school and Chloe won prizes for her art, and in the car Sue pointed out that a lot of the signs in the city said *Don't.*

"You've got to ignore them," said Sue. "*Don't go here, don't pick the wildflowers, no swimming, no standing*...don't listen. Or you'll never be brave."

And like many parents Sue seldom followed her own advice. She worked at a jewellery store in the mall and liked her hours and liked to pour a drink at five thirty. She didn't like to go to the garage because the sound of tools dropping on concrete made her jump and all she saw were opportunities for injury.

"What do you like about that place?" she asked Chloe in the car, and Chloe couldn't give a good answer. She closed her eyes briefly and saw wrenches hanging from hooks like icicles in some permanent Christmas, every object designed to solve a problem or make things better, her dad and uncle Frank so wise and able, and her days at the garage so different from those at school where the girls were changing friends every week.

"It's just fun," she said.

Daphnis noticed his hands getting stronger. He stopped needing help with tire irons and lug nuts and felt a thrill every time he used the wheel gun, that sound of speed and passing hilarity.

Frank and Charlie had one other mechanic, Shane Dorcon, and several part-timers who came and went. Daphnis liked to compete with their speed and strength.

He and Chloe both wanted to learn all they could about every car that came in.

In the summer holiday they sat outside the garage, to the side of it in the sun, resting their backs against the warm wall. They ate sandwiches and exaggerated truths and talked about kids they knew at school and in the neighbourhood.

By the water they watched sea lions barking at whatever it was they barked at, and bald eagles picking at salmon on the beach. And at the mall they bought Daphnis a pair of Chuck Taylors and a poster for Chloe's van, a painting of people with umbrellas in the sun having picnics on the grass and staring out at sailboats.

"That's like our summers," she said.

Daphnis saw the faces of customers when they got their bills, how they sometimes argued with Frank or Uncle Charlie, but he also sensed how happy most of them were to get their cars back, to know that screech of the fan belt was gone. A lot of people were proud of their cars, like the cars were pets or little kids or even heroes they looked up to. A guy came in with his old 911 all the time, which Daphnis was eventually allowed to work on. The man seemed to think the Porsche was an exact reflection of how well engineered he himself was, despite its constant flaws, and Daphnis respected that.

What Charlie and Frank didn't tell each other was that the young man from their shared dream would reappear at certain times in the dark as well as in daylight. He sometimes sat with Frank at a poker table. Frank loved gambling, and his favourite dreams had him scooping chips with both arms, hugging money like he hugged his wife and son. The young man would pat him on the back and smile. His eyes so charming, his manner so appealing but unsettling. "Go all in," he would say, and Frank would win the hand and hug the money.

Charlie, the more imaginative of the two, saw the fellow not only in his dreams but in the corner of his eye at work. He wore a suit like other young men wore—neatly cut, tight in all the right places. He was a little pudgy, in certain lights, but his appearance was immaculate and unmanning. Strangely relaxing, thought Charlie, sometimes.

The truth was—and he tried to be honest about this—Charlie admired women. He always had. Particular customers came into the shop, like Suzie-Marie or Mrs Barton, and he loved to make them smile. It was in those moments, just as he would ease into the joy and thrill of engaging with someone beautiful, that he would see the young man in the corner of his eye smiling.

Charlie turned his head, and of course there was no one there. He continued flirting with the women, and when they were gone he looked to his side and the young man reappeared. Once he got used to these apparitions Charlie wanted to smile back at him, but that was often when the young man was most repellent, after the women were gone. His knowing smile, his manner slightly unctuous, making Charlie feel guilty for needing so much beauty in his life.

He thought he was losing his mind, but after years of seeing him in so many corners of his life, he realized he wasn't crazy. He appeared to Frank and Charlie for different reasons and in different ways, and Charlie realized that the young man was Love. He turned up everywhere—sometimes when you needed him, otherwise when you neither expected nor wanted nor thought of him.

And more and more did Charlie notice Love spending time with the kids. Daphnis seventeen now and Chloe growing into that shape, even in her coveralls, that men and women have worshipped and chased and bottled in poems and wine.

One thing that Chloe discovered early was that she loved grease. She loved dipping her fingers and then her whole hands into the tubs of that honey-looking stuff, moving her fingers in the tub, the slip and resistance of it. Charlie got mad at her for leaving greasy prints all over the shop and spent too many months training her to keep her hands dry. "It's dangerous," he said.

It turned out that cleaning them was more so.

Pumice soap had a similarly sensual feel for her. Just as slippery but soft, the little bits of pumice—perhaps from ancient volcanoes—adding a ticklish grit to the fresh-smelling cream of the soap.

One day she was watching Daphnis leaning into the hood of a Volvo. His legs had grown so sturdy and his back seemed long and elegant. Everyone talked about what a smart and creative mechanic he was becoming.

It seemed to Chloe, as she watched him, that he'd become beautiful.

Because this was a garage, there were always fumes. Smells from oil and gas and cleaners and paint. Sometimes you walked in there and got knocked over by the chemicals in the air, but most of the time it was a more subtle intoxication, one you were barely aware of.

That's what Chloe attributed this feeling to, the fumes.

Daphnis used to seem like a brother to her.

She dipped her hands in grease and stared at him, touching her fingertips together lightly, pretending each opposing tip was his.

She walked over to Daphnis when he paused from his work and said, "Can you help me? Dad's always getting mad at my greasy fingers."

She gestured at the bottle of pumice soap, the Permatex Fast Orange Xtreme.

Daphnis didn't question why, for the first time, Chloe couldn't clean her own hands. He pumped a palmful of the liquid soap and took her by the fingertips, his first touch immediately sending a shiver up Chloe's nape and raising the delicate hair on her forearms.

He was neither rough nor businesslike nor dainty. Strong, familiar hands that suddenly did not feel so familiar. At first he rubbed the soap into both of her palms, the grit and cream breaking down the grease under a scent of springtime orange. And then he took one hand in both of his and she felt attended to, like a queen, the consistency now somewhere between silk and oil, and as he took each finger in his palms, he would have seen, if he had looked up, a gauze fall over her eyes on which were suspended drifting, transient shapes: peaches, horses, hot roses swelling and subsiding in a pool of milk. She was lost for a moment and then consciously opened her eyes and looked at his face while he concentrated on his business. His jaw strong and graceful, the slightest hint of ruthlessness in a crease between his eyebrows. Her friend, whom she had shared most secrets with.

"Better rinse off," he said.

The next day, she studied him again as he worked, how he smiled at something Frank had said, how he and Frank gently chastised Shane for something no doubt foolish.

Chloe wondered what it was that made Daphnis so beautiful. Was it his industry, his humour, some secret wisdom relayed by Frank and Lina?

Both children knew that their parents had adopted them, though not the exact circumstances. Both felt they had had the same upbringing, despite a few idiosyncrasies of each family. What was it that made Daphnis so compelling? What makes a person suddenly appear in a different light, the landscape blurring and disappearing around him?

These and other questions arose as her fingers searched deeper in a tub of grease.

When Shane and Frank went back to work, Chloe sheepishly appeared to Daphnis with her greasy hands held out.

"Sorry," she said.

This time she more consciously savoured his touch, letting that gauze hang longer.

She pushed up the sleeves of her coveralls to invite him farther up her arms. And when his hands enveloped that soft skin inside her wrists, higher towards her elbows, she couldn't restrain a sigh or gasp, a small, soft sound she had never made before.

Charlie looked through the window from the office to the shop floor and saw Chloe staring at Daphnis while Daphnis held her wrists. In the corner on a stool sat the young man, Love, with a cat on his lap, and the cat was blinking as he stroked its head.

Chloe spent the evening in her van, trying to draw but finishing nothing. Feeling sick but hungry, hot and cold. Restless. She rolled on her bed and rubbed her arms, punched her fists forward like she was shooting her sleeves, trying to make her skin burst off. She wanted to talk to someone, but her closest friend was Daphnis.

Should she tell him everything? Maybe living amidst these fumes wasn't healthy. Maybe she should go home and watch TV with her parents. But her home, even her parents, seemed so childish to her suddenly, so untuned to the truth and difficulties of living. Every drawing on the floor of her van was a partial sketch of Daphnis, the paper scattered there like leaves in a hopeless forest.

Now Shane, Shane Dorcon, was afflicted with the same disease. But he was older. He had already known love a few times. His apprenticeship as a mechanic was over. He was going to make some good coin soon, maybe land a top spot at a dealership, Mercedes or something, already had his own place. He had lived a lot for a young man, in fact, having fucked a travel agent ten years older, yet here he was in love with this fifteen-year-old girl.

More than a girl. "I don't know," he said. He seemed to say that to himself a lot. At the gym. In the shower. When he forgot where he last laid a tool. Her smile.

"I don't know."

He wanted to impress her. He wore tank tops under his coveralls and he let this be known. He undid the shirt portion and tied the sleeves at his waist, discreetly smearing grease under his deltoids to give them even more interest. When he leaned over an engine, he flexed his triceps and looked over his shoulder to see if she was looking.

She wasn't.

Since coming to the garage last year, he had known Daphnis and Chloe were inseparable. They acted like they were related, and at first Shane ignored them. Daphnis still showed no signs of needing to shave, and within the span of two weeks Shane Dorcon could sport a neck beard, a goatee, or a lumberjack, be any kind of man as regards the hair on his face.

The pair of them together had a kind of light around them, and if you were to ask Shane what the effect of that light might be, he would tell you, "I don't know."

And just as Daphnis appeared in a new way to Chloe, so did Chloe appear to Shane.

He brought them both little gifts at first, a Coke for Daphnis and a Snickers for Chloe. For her sixteenth birthday he bought Chloe a printed T-shirt with a girl in a bikini, smiling and leaning back on a '67 Mustang, and said, "It's nothing." He said to Daphnis, "We should go for a beer sometime. But you'll have to wear a fake beard or something."

All he wanted was to be with Chloe. She moved like a dancer or a hostess or a cat—he wasn't sure—and had a smile that made him calm and excited at the same time. There was something so innocent about her, like she didn't know much outside these walls.

He wanted to show her the world.

But he could never get her on her own, even for a moment. Once, when Daphnis was under a wheel, Shane thought about kicking out the jack. It's a quick way to go. He even looked around to see if anyone might notice.

But he realized the best way to get down Chloe's pants was to show her he was better than Daphnis, stronger, older.

One Friday he walked up to both of them and said, "Seriously. Let's go for that beer. I know a place where you guys won't get carded."

Chloe seemed the more excited of the two. That smile. She even wore the T-shirt that Shane had bought her, although Shane didn't know that, when she had first worn that shirt as a joke, Daphnis had stared at her. His eyes had gone to the woman on the car up to Chloe's face and down and up again and he said, "There should be a T-shirt with you on it."

Shane took them to his cousin's bar, the Rams, in the alley between Bastion and Wharf. Once upon a time it had been an inn for sailors and there was dark air in each of its corners that hadn't left the building since. The music was loud and the carpet wet with beer, and there was a pole on a stage in one corner that Chloe asked about.

"You don't know what that is?" Shane asked. "You'll see."

He ordered a pitcher and they sat at a table and he pounded back a glass. "Drink up," he said.

Daphnis had tried a beer with Frank at dinner sometimes, Chloe had smelled it and preferred ginger ale.

She lifted the beer to her mouth while Shane watched, took a smiling sip, wiped her lips with the back of her hand, and Shane thought, *God damn I could show her something.*

Daphnis sensed Dorcon's competitive spirit and felt up for any challenge. He and Chloe used to play the game in the back of her van, how long can you hold your breath. He was always good at it. He summoned that spirit and drank his beer very quickly.

"Ha," said Shane. "Let's have a battle. Wait here."

He went to the bar to get more beer and Daphnis and Chloe smiled at each other. She had another sip and thought about asking him a hundred questions, like what if we built a cabin by a lake and I slept every night with your golden hand on my back? And Daphnis felt some kind of energy rising, a force he later recognized as that in combustion engines, the same at the centre of the earth, the fire in each of us apportioned by the gods, in some not more than smoke and in some a conflagration, that gives this world its movement and thrum. He loved that dirty room and wanted to eat it. He loved her eyes that stared at him.

Shane came back holding the handles of two pitchers in each hand.

"Here's how it works," he said. He put the four pitchers on the table and said, "My friend here with the woman's face is going to prove to you that he is a man. And I am going to prove to you that I am a man. We'll match each other drink for drink and you, Chloe, have to drink two beers. And when you see that I'm better than him in every way, the winner gets to kiss you."

"What? Why do you make the rules?"

"Because I bought the beer."

The light changed in the bar suddenly, dimmer at first and then a spotlight swung around to the stage in the corner.

Over a loudspeaker came a voice that said, "Ladies and gentlemen, please put your hands together for Silver!"

Music pounded and to the stage strutted a woman in a grey-blue wig and silver thong. Daphnis felt a bit surprised and looked over his shoulder, as if he had walked into the wrong changing room.

Silver raised a strong and skinny arm and took hold of the pole like it was the neck of a rival. Her hips made an aggressive contraction and she leapt upside down on the pole, spun her legs as she descended, her thong giving a silver wink to the crowd. A table of men shouted, "Whoo!"

Shane filled three glasses and shouted, "Drink!"

The music was very loud and Chloe's thoughts had been disordered. What exactly was this game? Why should she care who was manly? What did drinking have to do with it? She knew whose lips she loved, whose lips she wanted to feel.

Silver stood rigid like a naked blade while the music held a beat, then spun wildly as the song turned manic. The two boys drank their beers as fast as they could. Shane was the quicker and proudly banged his glass on the table. He refilled it as Daphnis was finishing his.

Two more rounds were done this way, Shane smirking and removing his overshirt like he always did in the shop, now drinking in his tank top. He stared at Chloe and shouted, "Hot in here!"

She had drunk three-quarters of her glass and felt loose, like her bones were turning to rope.

"Say something!" she shouted over the music. "You guys have to say something! I don't care how much you can drink! I decide the winner!"

"Another round!" shouted Shane.

After five chugged beers, Daphnis was feeling gassy. He burped and then smothered another and the smothering made him feel ill.

"Another!" shouted Shane, and the table was wet with beer.

"Say something!" shouted Chloe again, and Shane said, "What?! Say what?!"

"I don't know! Tell me what you like about Silver!"

The three looked towards the stage.

Silver was making a waving motion from ankles to hips to head. She turned and whipped her blue hair and then leaned forward, far, opening herself to almost complete scrutiny.

"That's easy!" shouted Shane. "I don't like anything about her! She's a skank! Every biker in town has fucked her and that's her son over there, the fat one playing pool! Who brings her son to watch mommy strip?!"

He smiled at Chloe.

"I know what a beautiful girl is!" he shouted, and looked proud for knowing something.

He filled their glasses again and said, "Now you!" to Daphnis.

Still fired by the spirit of competition, Daphnis nonetheless realized he could never match Dorcon. The room moved a little like the horizon on those days he went fishing with Frank.

"Tell your sister what you like about the stripper!"

Silver was doing the splits, which was impressive to Daphnis. The spotlight swung around and exaggerated the movement of the room and it shone on Silver's haunches as he watched her stand and hook her thumbs in her thong and slide it down.

He had never seen a naked woman outside of pictures. Everything seemed blue and cold for a moment, like this was all taking place under moonlight. A priestess whom he was meant to worship revealing her shaved blue secret. What a lonely world must the moon look down upon, the frightened souls who can't sleep.

She suddenly seemed so strong to Daphnis, to dance while showing so much. "She's doing what she can," he said.

"What?!" shouted Shane.

"She's doing what she can!"

The room gave a lurch.

Chloe stared at him and stood and leaned over the table. She took his beautiful face in her hands and kissed those lips she had dreamt of. A simple kiss, lips a little cooled by beer yet hot as a cattleman's brand.

In that moment Daphnis awakened, transformed, and left a boy behind who had never seen how richly soaked the reds and pinks of this world could be, how deep the velvet of a petal.

The rest of the night was a blur except for that kiss. He couldn't remember going to the bathroom, couldn't remember how long he stayed.

He couldn't have known how heated Dorcon's bones had grown, the sight of Silver's flesh, however repulsive he pretended it was, the size of Chloe's eyes as she looked at Daphnis and kissed him. Dorcon wanted to fight everyone in that bar, and he put his hand on Chloe's thigh while Daphnis was in the bathroom.

"Come home with me," he said.

Moved his hand up higher and squeezed until she flinched.

"Come home with me."

From the bar a man who called himself Coyote told his friend to turn and watch. "Looks like Shane's got himself a little meal."

"I'd wake up to that," said the friend.

In the bathroom, Daphnis tried to understand what was happening to him. The room was spinning and he felt sick from all the beer. Thoughts of Chloe shining and fading and he rested his head on the cubicle wall.

"Come home with me," said Shane again, and it felt to Chloe now like he was giving her no choice.

A new feeling, this fear. Her body in the hands of some force greater than Shane, something in and around him that even he had little control over. Another dancer appeared onstage, nude without preliminaries, and the bar had filled, the music louder to overcome the shouts of customers.

"I want to wait for Daphnis."

"He's not invited," said Shane. "Let's just go."

"Is there a way out the back?"

"By the bathroom," he said. He got excited.

"I'll go to the bathroom and I'll meet you out back," said Chloe.

Coyote watched them stand together and he came and put his hand on Shane's shoulder. They talked while Chloe slipped through to the bathroom, through a crowded corridor where packages were exchanged and a man and woman fought about having no money, no promise, no love left to give them any comfort.

Chloe went into the men's bathroom and banged on each of the doors.

She shook her love by the shoulders and said, "We have to go, now!"

And Daphnis rode the seas. Sailed along a vast dark shore where people shouted and a Siren twisted naked like a snake. Through a cloud of beer that made him retch and the hands of a smiling man who said, "Your girlfriend gets around!"

Chloe was trying to support his weight, expecting Shane to appear or to feel his hand again. That smiling man was watching her, his ears tattooed and his friend wearing a Jokers biker jacket.

At the back of the bar, in the parking lot, Dorcon waited.

Joints and pipes were smoked and a dancer said, "It's too fuckin hot in there." And Dorcon felt his heart leap every time the back door opened.

In the locker room, Silver had wiped her armpits and removed her wig, taken off her makeup. She scratched her short hair, put trousers on and a suit, and she smiled. Watched herself transform. The suit was tight in all the right places, maybe too tight. If you had been standing outside that door, you might have seen a middle-aged woman go into the locker room and a well-dressed young man come out.

He winked. He walked past the fighting couple and out into the bar, where he found a place in one of the dark corners, watching the other dancers, watching everything as a dance.

In the morning, Daphnis was in pain. Not in his head or in his stomach but in his heart. It seemed ridiculous, unreasonable, that a kiss, especially one so simple, could change the world and put the moon and the sun together in the sky so that when he slept he was wide awake and asleep as he moved through the day. All he could think about was that kiss and Chloe's eyes before and after she gave it. As if he himself had not had eyes before last night, had not been able to see how beautiful his friend was. This girl he had grown up with, her laugh and kindness so constant, those eyes now explaining why sapphires, diamonds, pearls ever had any value. We searched for jewels because they reminded us of her eyes.

And just as Chloe had writhed in pain in her van, Daphnis now did the same in his bed at home. Wanting her company, afraid of how little strength he would have around her. Those soft and honest lips an invitation to a world so much bigger than this, a world he wanted but perhaps was not prepared for.

He had thought of Chloe as younger, but now she seemed to be ahead of him, daring him to catch up.

Shane Dorcon was angry. He'd won the drinking game but didn't get the kiss. He'd been promised that she would come home with him, and he waited in that parking lot for twenty minutes. He thought about telling Charlie he was going to quit, knowing it would fuck him up because mechanics were hard to find these days, especially good ones like Shane.

He actually had a lot of knowledge, secrets about that family. He knew Charlie didn't trust banks and kept big money in the safe in the office. His cousin who owned the Rams was tight with bikers, the Jokers, and Shane worked on their bikes sometimes on weekends. Last night Coyote said, "Keep an eye on that girl you're with or she'll never see outside a motel."

Summer was as swollen as it could be. The ocean warm, the forests thick.

Daphnis and Chloe drove Frank's truck up the coast like they'd done last year, to swim near the park where the cedars leaned over the water. They'd been so many times as kids, mostly with parents and then without—last year being the first time they drove on their own, when

Daphnis still had his learner's permit and shouldn't have been on the highway.

The air in the cab of that truck was hung with candy and questions. Every time one of them shifted, even raising a finger to scratch a forehead, the other hoped it would move them closer. Each of them ached to be touching, to say something that would give them permission to pull over and submit.

"What do you want to listen to?"

"Anything. What do you want to listen to?"

There was a smile around every word.

At the water was a rock that they had called their own for years. It had a flat top like a table, where they could lay a few towels, get warmed by the sun, and jump from, eight feet above the surface. Daphnis ran to it from the truck, needing that water to give him reason and sense, something cool to calm him. He ran so fast that from the water he could look back and watch her arrive.

She had such grace, her dress loose and white.

They had long noticed changes in each other's body, of course, but they used to be the source of jokes.

Nothing could now be more serious.

He watched her lift her dress by the hem and felt too shy to look.

But he did.

Prayers came up in whispers from the water. That she would be happy. That they would be together. An inarticulate prayer beyond the words within his reach that if he should find the courage to cleave life's fictions and stare at whatever fire lay beyond them, that holding hands or dying alone they would always love the burning.

On the shore she thought of him. His clothes lay on the rock and she took his T-shirt and put it on, waited for him to come back, and she closed her eyes and lay in the sun feeling the warm rock on the backs of her legs. A shadow came across her eyes and she opened them, and Daphnis was standing over her.

A grasshopper had been nestled in his shirt before she'd put it on and she suddenly felt its tickle. She was startled and the grasshopper kept trying to leap out.

"Get it!" she said, and they both had their hands down the front of his big T-shirt, trying to get the grasshopper but holding hands instead, their forearms touching on her belly and both of them laughing.

The grasshopper jumped away and stared sideways from the rock and a cardinal, blue jay, swallow, and crow all had eyes on it for a meal.

Had Daphnis known that there was always something over his shoulder, a thief, a rival, he might have done everything more urgently, but summer was at its height that day and it seemed there was nothing but time.

He picked up the grasshopper and Chloe said, "Don't you dare!" She laughed and half-heartedly fought him off, and the grasshopper was soon down her shirt again, ticklish and prickly.

She took off his T-shirt and stood and jumped from the rock into the water in a way that told him to chase her.

Daphnis jumped and they were the only two in that shaded inlet, everything warm with promise.

Do you remember that day, my fellow old fools, as you limp on broken knees?

The world is ahead, just there: She is taking a mouthful of water, a fount, and you can touch her but you don't, because there is time, that day, there was time.

They swam on their backs, the water like warm cream, and they thought of nothing. They laughed and swam closer and on the rock they kissed again, this time longer, mouths open.

And in the autumn old men would make wine.

The summer passed with nights of aching, days of swimming and working and smiles. Her van the site of some of Love's most nectarine moments.

"You're my best friend," she said.

"Do you remember those books I used to read about pirates?" said Daphnis. "The ones who stole people. They raided other countries and took everything, you know, wheat and clothes. Countries that didn't have treasure? And they realized that people were the valuable things. Everyone's valuable to someone.

"Stealing people and selling them back, taking them somewhere else and selling them.

"I remember wondering, what if I got taken? What if pirates came in here and took me?"

They sat on her bed in the van in the garage and she ran her fingers through his hair while he talked.

"And I'm thinking, I *have* been taken," he said. "You're the only thing I think about."

She kissed him on the forehead and cheeks, on the lips and on his neck, on his arms and on his lips again, and that kiss was a deep one.

BOOK TWO

Frank and Charlie made homemade wine and threw a party every September. The following year was their biggest. They invited parents and neighbours and kids who were friends with their kids, who were looking less like kids, and few people were truthful about how bad their wine was.

Frank poured a glass for Lina before the party and stared at her. Sometimes the quietest of them all, she came alive at the end of each summer and was eager to show her garden to everyone. Frank had a bigger yard than Charlie, and Lina worked on it every day.

"If I was a stranger, I'd ask for your number," said Charlie.

"That's my wife," said Frank.

"I'd just be calling... getting advice on the garden and whatnot."

Chloe wore a tight green dress that she felt good in, which suggested to many that summer wouldn't end this year. Frank's neighbour, Greg Lampis, put his arm over her shoulder and said, “Now that you’re fixing cars, I’ll drive mine into a wall.”

In fact, most of the men at the party had leaping goats in their hearts and made a point of touching Chloe’s fingers when she handed them glasses of wine.

“They’re sure growing up,” said several people that day.

Daphnis was cornered by girls from school. Darlene Sweet, who had also turned eighteen, showed him the word *sweet* that had been freshly tattooed pretty low on her right breast.

“That looks nice,” said Daphnis, quite honestly.

There was a point at that party every year where most people stopped realizing how bad the wine was. Evening came and lanterns were lit and everyone, consciously or not, began loudly defying the darkness.

And the darkness had been gathering for years.

Across that city a disease had spread and left poverty in its wake. Many of Frank and Charlie’s friends could no longer afford their houses. Only the rich seemed able to carry on and they only seemed to get richer.

The business at the garage was safe for now because rich people still drove cars and cars would always break down, but food was expensive, the kids were expensive, and as much as this party was to celebrate a harvest, the baskets around that city were light.

Frank drank too much and tripped on a paving stone. Spilled wine on his shirt and said to Charlie, “You can’t talk about my wife like that. The jokes about calling her. She's my wife."

"Fuck you, Frank, I'm only joking. She's got a glow. Be proud."

"Fuck you. I am proud. No one's taking anything." He swept his arm across the night like a drunken king. "It's all mine," he said.

Daphnis stole a kiss from Chloe, and Lina came and kissed Charlie and said, "Stop being a dog." She took Daphnis's hand and said, "Go look at my garden, you two."

They passed Lina's moonflowers and lanterns and a bower and Chloe spotted someone she knew, a retired old lawyer named Phil Philetas whom she had always liked.

"Hi, Mr Philetas," she said.

What a sad old face he had, and what a change when he looked up and saw them.

His wife had died two years ago.

He always liked to tell stories.

Phil had fought for most of these people, getting them off traffic charges, helping with injury and small claims. For decades he had been at least elbow-deep in their tragedies and cheats.

"I like sitting in this garden," he said. "Sit down with me for a second. My wife used to plant flowers. Do you know that?"

"No," said Chloe.

She sat on a bench with him while Daphnis stood.

"We have a big garden," said Phil. "We have a big house. A mansion. I sit there all alone in it, these days. And sometimes I go out into the garden. My wife was like your mom, Daphnis. Always out there watering, pruning. Amaryllis was her favourite flower. I stared at them for hours this summer. When they die, their petals hang down like this. Like an old lady's hair after a shower," he said.

"You can learn a lot from death. You could have looked at me up there in my mansion, lifetime in the law, and you could say that must be a wise man up there. But I didn't know anything until she died. How much death there is in life. How alive she still is.

"Never a religious man, but I see signs and wonders these days.

"Just yesterday... Let me tell you a story... Just yesterday I was staring out at the garden and I saw a young man wandering through it. On my property.

"I stood up, I won't show you, with a drink in my hand, and I opened the back door. Said, 'Hey, who are you?! What are you doing here?!' Young guy. Well-dressed. Thought he might have been a client.

"'Do I know you?!'

"'Of course!' he says.

"I'm walking over to him and he's standing in the middle of my wife's dead flowers.

"'You have to cut the heads off,' he says. 'Or they'll never live again.'

"I couldn't remember where exactly I knew him from, but he was familiar. Nice guy. Nice-looking. And next thing I know, I'm having a drink with him in the living room.

"We talked about everything, the law, politics. I like to move my mouth, otherwise there's too much time to think, and I said that, I said, 'I don't like thinking these days, the loneliness of it,' and he said, 'That's everyone's problem. No one likes being sad these days. No one ever did, but it's worse now than ever . . .'

"Do you see what he was saying?"

"No," said Daphnis.

"No. Well, if you get busy and work your tail off, work as a lawyer, say, twelve hours a day, all in the name of making money, providing, preparing . . . you think you're living, you think you're alive and struggling, that you're avoiding sadness and loneliness and boredom and death, but it's really just Death winning. Do you see?"

"No," said Daphnis.

"Anyway, the young man said the world is distracting itself to death, and I couldn't have agreed more, and as I'm talking he interrupts me and says, 'I used to see the way you looked at your wife'."

Phil stopped looking at Daphnis and Chloe and stared out warmly as if he was seeing a face beyond the lantern.

"'I was there,' he says. 'And when you looked at her, you weren't talking. You weren't working. You were in love,' he says."

He turned to them again and said, "Do you see?"

He had a plaintive look.

Daphnis and Chloe liked Mr Philetas but quietly decided that he'd had too much wine.

"He wasn't even there, the young man. I put my drink down and he wasn't even there. Signs and wonders. But his point stayed with me, you see. His point was you two should be looking at each other. If there's love, there's calm, and death will never win."

Lina thought of her son's powerful hands and remembered when she first met Frank, how funny he was and strong. She peeled an orange over the garbage and thought that's all life does. Puts a peel on us. A thicker layer of skin and wrinkles, but underneath there's still the same fruit. She looked back at the years of raising Daphnis, the different ages, the diapers and days before school, looking over her shoulder for someone trying to take him. Hoping he'd be a better version of herself and trying to let him be. Always worrying and burying the worry. The peel getting thicker all the time. She couldn't see her real self when she looked in the mirror, but she could see the real Frank, the real Daphnis, when she looked at them, Frank stooping and distracted but strong inside, the light still in his eyes. Felt like they had lived a couple of lifetimes and the fruit was still there and sweet.

Another spring and summer passed.

Chloe taller than Sue and she came into the store at the mall looking confident, her smile like that of other ring-buyers, the affianced, but still the girl Sue knew, her Chloe, more interested in wrenches than in rings.

"I'm guessing you're not going to buy anything."

"Let's go for coffee."

"Coffee? I didn't drink coffee till I was thirty."

"But you drank beer when you were twelve."

Sue felt that motherhood was increasingly about standing back and watching, even turning her back and having faith that those square shoulders were getting strong enough now to bear anything.

Lina met Chloe and Sue for coffee and they walked, and the older women stayed back a few steps.

Lina asked Sue if she could remember how old she was when she stopped skipping.

Daphnis and Chloe were never happy unless they were looking at each other.

They both made excuses in the evenings and met up in Chloe's van in the garage, taking one step further every night towards that satisfaction that true lovers will simply never find.

But even as the light in Daphnis and Chloe grew, the darkness over the city deepened.

Frank had been gambling too much.

Not just at cards but on sports. Taking Lina on a cheap flight to Vegas once and behaving as if it was all good fun, but at every waking moment and often through his dreams he thought of nothing but chasing a win or how much he had lost. Lina asked if they could just have dinner one night and see a show, and they did; but he ended up at the sportsbook after watching her fall asleep.

He refinanced their house and pretended to the bank that he needed new equipment for the garage. He put money in stocks and the stock market collapsed in the wake of the disease.

Frank had no money.

He knew that Charlie kept a lot in the safe in the office and had stood over his shoulder often. Charlie was his best friend, but there are times through the night, should you live long enough, where you realize everything but survival is a word.

Friend.

Loyalty.

Family.

Wife.

Just words if the wolves are standing over you.

I'm alone, thought Frank.

For years they had fixed the cars of shady people. Sometimes the nicer the car, the greater the cheat. He and Charlie had never cared, a car was a car. Shane brought in the Harleys of his biker friends, and Coyote came in with a Mercedes and a Lexus.

"How do you do it? Make all this money?" Frank asked him.

Coyote smiled. "I'm like a bank. That's all. Except I offer more than a bank does. Not just money. I care," he said, still smiling. "Banks don't give a shit, but I do. You want this, I'll give you this, you want that, I'll give you that. Help you find it. Life's about building castles."

Frank knew he ran girls and drugs, and his tattoos could make him look like someone you shouldn't get close to. But when he talked, he seemed smart. Didn't wear the clothes of a biker, the patches and the Joker jacket—dressed like a businessman, in suits and polo shirts. You didn't even notice his tattooed ears because his eyes were bright—like he had a joke to tell or wisdom you could ask about.

"I'm impressed with anyone makes money these days," said Frank. "I don't judge. I work hard and never got over that hump, myself, but I don't judge."

"Judging's for weaklings and women," said Coyote.

Frank had done well with the garage, but they were never going to make the big money, the kind that meant Daphnis could go to university. Buy a house for his boy. Not just take the worry out of life but hold on to a little gold. That work he and Charlie had done, the fumes and the grease and the fingernails missing. When he awoke and couldn't breathe every morning at three, while everyone else in the house was asleep, he stared at his mechanic's hands in the bathroom and knew his choices in life had run out.

At first Coyote said, "I'll pay your loans with the bank. Think of me like them except once your money's with me, I won't hassle you with the letters and the phone. If you want more, I won't ask questions. I know you're good for it."

That last line meant a lot to Frank.

When the world has left you on the side of the road, how much does it mean when someone pulls over, pays a little compliment? Frank thought about picking up the baby Daphnis from the sidewalk. And all the sacrifices he'd made for Lina. He needed a little help.

Coyote didn't want much at first. Some freebies at the garage, tire changes, brakes. When Frank was free of the bank, he used this new business arrangement as a reality check, a kind of restart. *Don't take more from Coyote,* he told himself. Just rebuild. Smart bets only.

Coyote charged the same rate as the bank for the first hundred thousand. Then an extra point. Three points. Eight.

Frank brought cash to the Jokers' clubhouse once a month, meeting Coyote in the office or at the bar. Coyote often sat with a youth, a young man, a different one each time. Holding his hand across the bar, leaning over to kiss him. Coyote was warm in greeting Frank and warm with whoever his friend was, sitting at the corner bench in the clubhouse with his lover's head on his shoulder, tender lips on his forehead.

If you looked at the lot outside the garage, you'd think business was good. Not only a lot of cars, but nice cars. Escalades and BMWs, a tricked-out F-150.

Frank thought about how much he and guys like him struggled and he couldn't believe the wealth of some of these others, a few of them not much older than Daphnis. The young ones with the Escalades all looked the same—hair shaved close on the sides, jewellery, puffed up with steroids.

You hit a low and think *I've never felt so low* and then you hit a lower low and think you were a fool for thinking you had been low. *This* is the lowest I've been, you say to that face in the mirror, and next you can't even bear to look.

Frank lay down on the floor of the bathroom and thought, *I've been so goddamn stupid.*

He'd told Daphnis that school didn't matter, there was too much work at the shop. He and Daphnis made secret compartments in doors, hydraulic lifts hidden in centre consoles. Places where guns and drugs could be hidden.

A guy named Bryan came in all the time with different cars. His own was a Lincoln SUV with a cage in the back for two Neapolitan mastiffs that Frank had built for free.

Over eighteen months they rebuilt most of the gang's cars, and Frank chased solutions at the book or in cards.

Six hundred thousand in debt to Coyote, no equity left in the house or business, the shop controlled by gangsters. He even borrowed money from Dorcon, who made Frank double his wage.

Charlie wondered why they were so busy and not seeing profit and Frank started drinking more to calm his nerves. Rye at midnight in the garage at home, his hand shaking until the drink brought him a couple of hours of calm.

Daphnis came out to him one night and said, "What's wrong, Dad? You're skinny."

"I'm okay."

"Why are you drinking out here?"

"I'm just thinking, you know. Didn't want to wake you guys."

Daphnis unfolded a lawn chair and sat with him.

Quiet for a moment and Frank looked at Daphnis, a man now.

"You're smarter than me," Frank said. "Smarter and all grown up. I'm not worried about you."

"You don't need to worry about me."

"I'm not."

"So what are you worried about?"

"I don't know. You get old, you worry."

"Well... Don't. You'll get too skinny."

"I won't."

"I love you, Dad."

Frank cried about that later. Held his own head in his stained and loathsome hands and thought for a brief and blessed moment that maybe he hadn't failed.

Daphnis watched the cars come and go from the shop. Each more than a hundred grand.

Dudes in flip-flops and Cartier watches.

He had been going to a boxing gym for a couple of years, and his coach said, "I'll tell you something most fighters never learn. You hear people say, 'I'm a lover not a fighter,' but the best fighters are lovers too."

He explained what he meant in little lessons, simple sayings like, "Fight with a full heart.

"The more blood in your body, the heavier your punches."

His basic theory was if you love someone then you know what they want, and if you know what someone wants you'll know how to fight them.

His coach stood behind Daphnis in his daydreams.

"The best fighters see everything. They're above the fight. You can't see everything if you don't know how to love. Now box!"

These young guys with the cars, some of them weren't obvious bikers like Shane's crowd. They copied Coyote. Bryan with the mastiffs looked like a gangster—a tough guy—but not a biker. Came up through some affiliate crew that Coyote folded in with the Jokers, and Bryan and his boys wore black suits on Friday nights and started fights in bars.

Coyote set them up in apartments around the city where they ran dial-a-dopes. Bryan was Coyote's top soldier who did a lot of the dirty work but had his own hierarchy beneath him. Group of guys who mostly sold fentanyl and meth.

Daphnis saw Bryan talking to Frank one day in the shop, shoulders all roided and poking at Frank's chest with two fingers. Daphnis wiped his hands on a rag and heard his boxing coach behind him saying, "Love him, Daphnis. Look at that bully and love him. What do you think he wants?"

Daphnis saw his dad looking thin and cowering and he understood that the bully and the bullied are the same, they both just want to be loved.

He wore a small smile, unafraid.

"What's going on?"

"The pretty boy," said Bryan.

"My son," said Frank.

"Here to help, is he?"

"He's a good boy. It's okay, D. Just get back to work."

"What does he want, Dad?"

"What do I want? I want your dad to do his fuckin job. I need my car. What do you want, tough guy? You're gonna work here till you're old and weak?"

"My dad's not weak."

"No, eh? I'll tell you what."

He squared up to Daphnis wrapping a dog leash around his fists and pulling it taut. "I'm just the needle.

It's the stuff behind me you worry about. Picture this, daddy. Your good-looking boy here, strong, with this leash around his wrists and thirty guys beating on his face. Weak or strong, he'll never walk again. Right?"

Daphnis kept smiling. *He just wants to be loved,* he thought.

Bryan wore a beard and a face that never changed.

"You're a good boy, D." Frank put an arm between them. "Go back to work."

"How bad?" asked Lina in bed.

Bad enough that Frank couldn't speak without feeling sick.

Charlie could have killed him.

Lina could have left him.

Everyone could have hated him. But they didn't. They loved Frank.

Money was a capricious and vengeful god, unkind even to those who worshipped him.

Money will haunt every thought, every hope, make you do things a reasonable person would never do, throw decades away in his name.

Daphnis and Chloe often talked about where they might go, what they might do.

"Do you want to travel?"

"Yeah."

"Where to?"

"Everywhere."

"With kids?"

"Ten."

"Will they look like you?"

"I hope they look like you."

"Will we need a big house?"

"All I need is this van."

"So where do you want to go in it?"

"Right here."

The battle of gods that will never end was that between Love and Money.

"I need to help Dad," said Daphnis. "I need to make more money."

He had a childish understanding of Frank's problem at first, thinking if he saved a little, chipped in...

But it became more clear to him that the problem was big. Bags of coke and pills out in the open and getting stashed behind door panels, the cars coming and going outside regular hours.

"It's too much," said Charlie. "I don't need police." He was despondent, angry, more willing to offend Coyote and the others, and then one day he too was silent, compliant. Looking squarely back at Coyote, who stared at him from a corner of the garage. A smirk from the biker that somehow made everything in Charlie's life feel temporary.

It was a troubling step towards adulthood for Daphnis to see his uncle and father, former kings of his world, looking so cowed and obeisant.

One of Bryan's meth dealers came in with his Honda Civic, his turbo exhaust not tuned like he liked. Skinny, arrogant kid who was put on this earth to jeer and make noise.

Chloe was under his car and the guy was looking at her hips and legs and biting the knuckles of his pointer.

Something rose up in Daphnis. The thought of turbo pipes whistling and popping, the bikes roaring around the streets all day, and everyone, always, looking at Chloe. He knew some kind of filth was going to come from this loser's mouth, so he went over and simply stopped it. Not a sucker punch, but not much warning either.

The guy was on the floor, smile like the devil's piano with blood between his teeth.

"You're so fuckin dead."

He picked up a flashlight and swung it, clipping just enough of Daphnis's nose to break it.

Daphnis gave him the one-two, what his coach called the 12-train, medium jab to his jaw as a distraction then the right to knock him out.

Chloe was crying and trying to stop the blood from Daphnis's nose and the guy was out cold on the floor.

"Get out of here," said Frank. "Both of you. Go."

Chloe took him to the hospital. Washed his face with wipes in the waiting room before he had his nose reset.

"I love you," she said. "I love you, I love you, I love you."

The next day, Coyote tapped him on the shoulder.

"We should talk."

He was taller than Daphnis and equally broad, and beneath his suit were coils of intelligent menace. Except for his tattooed ears you might think he was one of those motivational speakers, a big presence on a stage with hands and a smile that could persuade you to do anything.

"Is she your girlfriend or your sister?"

"She's everything."

"She was disrespected. I get it. But you can't punch my guys. You punch my guys and you will get punched back." He put his hands on Daphnis's shoulders and Daphnis didn't know if a hit was coming. "The only time you can give them a smack is if you are one of my guys too. If you're with me, you can beat the shit out of anyone. I hear you've got a solid swing."

He kept his hands on Daphnis as if feeling for strength. Looked him deeply in the eye.

"Join us. Think about it." He stepped away and looked around. "I don't know what you're gonna do to make things right today, though. He's got a concussion and a broken tooth."

"I'll fix the exhaust. Give him a tune-up."

"Yes, you will. This place isn't going to last if you guys keep working for free. Think about what I said."

Daphnis didn't take long.

He went to an apartment in South End where they stashed and cut drugs and counted money past midnight.

"Learn the ropes," said Coyote.

They had a list of a couple of hundred clients and those clients all had one number to call whenever they wanted anything. Those calls were forwarded to dialers by a dispatcher at the apartment and the dialers called back with requests, mostly fentanyl and cocaine.

At the apartment, a couple of guys cut the drugs with caffeine and organized the bags for each order, and the dialers came and got the bags and delivered to apartments and agreed-upon drops: Harbour Pizza, the Quality Inn, the campground at Living Forest.

See it from above as the gods do. Young men on bikes and scooters flying out from the building on Seventh, little bees with buzz and purpose. They spread joy and oblivion across the city and return with bags of nectar. How happy is Love to see the girls get lines to sniff at the Quality Inn, the passion they show thereafter. And Money smiling, fat, in the apartment on top of the stash house.

Daphnis didn't tell Chloe he was looking in on this life. Trying it out. Getting money from Coyote was a kind of revenge. Maybe there was some way out for all of them.

"Everything is going to be great," he said.

His boxing coach called and said, "We haven't seen you in a while."

"I know. I'm busy."

"Good fighters see it all. Don't forget that."

Coyote loaned him a red '97 Super Hawk, his for five grand if he wanted. "It's the poor man's Ducati."

He'd ridden a bike before but nothing that fast. He did the routes to the regular drops, hours of constant movement and doing his best to keep the motorbike under the limit. Kept his helmet on so clients never saw him, and his head was on a swivel for the cops.

Days at the shop and nights on the streets, he didn't see Chloe enough. He tried to tell her that everything he did he did for Love and that her face was always behind his eyes and her face was the thing that told him that everything was going to be great.

Chloe stayed in school, learning the ever-broadening array of things that have nothing to do with love or life or enlightenment, the noise and judgments that put us in the way of each other and seldom speak to the ache and hunger for beauty, the ache that made Dorcon and all his buddies plot over how to get Chloe alone.

She felt some days that she had a choice to make: to see the world either as a threat or as full of possibility. Hide her body or pull her shoulders back.

She got up early to get ready for school, stood in front of the mirror to put her earrings on.

How do you know how to be when you don't yet know who you are, and what if who you are is just an idea in someone else's eyes? And what about this feeling, that she's a shell when she's not with Daphnis, how lost and found she feels when she's with him?

Daphnis said, "I'm making money."

"I want to make money," she said.

"Keep studying. You're smarter than me."

"Maybe my mom could steal from the store. It gets robbed all the time. We could give them jewellery. How much does your dad owe?"

"More than that."

"I want to help."

"You do. You make everything beautiful. I feel it. I feel it whenever I'm with you. When I think about... I ride a bike sometimes these days... Getting to know motorbikes. And it's like I'm riding after you, chasing you. You're up ahead. All the answers. They're up ahead. They're in you. Do you feel it? How fast it feels?"

"I feel it," she said.

The money was pretty good. There was more to make if you cut the drugs or got on dispatch or if you rose closer to Bryan and ran a crew.

Bryan watched Daphnis with distrust.

Too clean.

How did a blond kid, daddy's boy, suddenly get in with them? Never held a gun or been arrested, never known what it was like to walk past genuine corners.

"Come out with us," he said. "Get yourself a suit and come out Friday."

He didn't want to belong, Daphnis. He didn't need to be part of a gang or any group. What he wanted was Chloe, and freedom. To dive underwater with her on a hot summer day and stay suspended until the last second. To kick his legs to the surface and breathe her in, hold her, take her to the rock and lie down.

"We'll live forever," he said once. "I know it. I'll love your face forever."

He needed money to get Frank and Charlie free. He needed money to put gas in Chloe's van and drive to who knows where, over the mountains to the other coast.

He bought a black suit and felt itchy in it, met Bryan and a gang of ten others at the Terminal Bar near the city harbour.

The purpose of Friday nights was to fight. Jokers versus the United Nations. The West End Boys. Sometimes outnumbered, sometimes in the majority. Spilling into the parking lot. That night at the Terminal Bar there was a bunch of UN guys with their girlfriends, already playing pool.

The fights were battles over dealing spots or supply, part of bigger wars over turf. Smaller gangs fighting to be noticed and taken in, absorbed by Coyote or the Hells.

Bryan made Daphnis start it. One of the UN guys had already made fun of their suits, saying, "Here come the waiters," when they first walked in.

Their girls doing shots at the bar and laughing.

Bryan's girlfriend Jenna was there, older than Bryan and unfriendly. She looked at Daphnis with fear or recognition, a reflexive hostility to someone who looked like he did.

"Show us you can fight," said Bryan, "and we'll see." He handed Daphnis a beer. "Lots of other jobs."

Daphnis drank and felt himself go into a trance, above it all like his coach told him but a different feeling from any sparring he'd done. The same pump of blood, but there was some kind of poison in it. He didn't want to fight, but once it started it felt more like life or death than any fight he'd been in.

Some other guy with a name and life, somebody's son. Daphnis was told he should hate him. Hate his face. Fuck him up. The guy held Daphnis by the collar with his left, yanking it down like this was a hockey fight. Daphnis had a longer reach and the guy was down after three punches, his fingers limp but hooked enough into Daphnis's collar that he dragged him down as he collapsed.

He felt a sharp, hot slap on his ear, pain chasing it, pain like he had never felt, and he was staring at the ceiling. One of the others had hit him with a pool cue and was now standing over him.

Bryan had spiked Daphnis's beer with ketamine to see how he would deal with the float, learn what life is like when the ground gives way and your daddy can't protect you. And float is what Daphnis did, through a shipwreck where sailors fought each other for breath, dragging each other under a burning sea. Jenna ripped a handful of hair out of the head of another girl and the screaming is all that Daphnis remembered, the constant desperate screech of a terrified chimpanzee.

Lina said to Sue one night when the kids were little, "It's a miracle any of us make it." Pinching loose skin on the back of her hand after putting a Band-Aid on Daphnis. Trying to articulate as we stare at our children how many thousands of murderers and thieves have to be passed before this journey even reaches noon. "You'll be fine," she said to her son.

Daphnis got a bump up to doing dispatch, a simple job of forwarding calls to the riders, the riders calling back with orders, telling the guys in the apartment how much to measure into bags. A middle manager's role and he got more money.

But it didn't last.

"Coyote wants you back on the street," said Bryan. He wanted Daphnis in jeopardy. "You can have your little red bike again."

No awareness yet in Daphnis of the writhing amniotes behind Coyote's eyes, the heat and wet spawn and the lightning that sent him to the throats of beautiful men.

When Daphnis got the calls, it was the same voice every time from a different mouth.

"I need Chinese."

"I need some dirty."

The voice of someone who's lost his job, lost his purpose, lost her daughter to the drug that's killing her now. There's a wind up there that has blown out all the candles, blown away hope and joy, and what is left is only that same voice, "I'm alive, so help me die."

Daphnis rode the motorbike to apartments around the city. Coke to the partiers, to other bikers, fentanyl to the guy he recognized from TV football. Sometimes the bags he handed over seemed like little opportunities for people to love life again.

O, Love.

He sent Chloe texts with hearts and peeled bananas, eggplants and peaches. If a wind has blown out candles, there's another over the mountains that will carry sparks and fire. Daphnis was its messenger.

Chloe tried to draw every thought she had, every want. She wanted to see so much, and as she moved her pencil she realized she had seen so little. Deciding to pull her shoulders back and open her eyes to everyone, to lives she couldn't fathom, on the bus, smiling at the lonely-looking man who sold hot dogs by the harbour.

She skipped school one day and wandered through the small downtown, the cinema boarded over and the variety store playing loud music over a streetfront of

T-shirts and plastic jewels. Morning rain steaming on the streets. Off Bastion were a couple of little lanes with galleries, some just tourist shops but one that she had sometimes wondered about. Photos and paintings in the window. It was expensive-looking art, but there was still something inviting about the place.

She was anxious opening the gallery door, especially when she realized she was the only visitor in a fairly dark room. Not there to buy, not sure at all why she was there.

A bald man whose remaining hair was long on the sides and back said, "Hi," as he sat behind a half wall. The only light in the room came from above each artwork and from a word over the door in lit fluorescent tubing: *Wildlife*. The work of two artists—a photographer and a painter—hung separately over each half of the room.

Chloe felt watched, uncertain, not knowing how to look or where to begin, but she knew that red was the colour that will always summon the eyes and she walked to a painting of a red sky over farmland where a dragon and sheep lay sleeping.

The paintings were all of fantastical scenes, in oil, most the size of her bathroom mirror. A painting of a maypole on a city street, dancers leaping under a melancholy sky.

A man and woman walked towards a distant cave where smoke was emerging, either a refuge or a trap, and in another painting a woman in purple poured an amphora from which a river flowed, a source, and a white-bearded deity sat in grey robes presiding over the foreground with a sleeping pig at his feet. Another sad sky with a hint of hope, in orange, the scene both rich and bleak, which surely came from the painter dipping a brush in his own bruises.

The photos, by the other artist, were mostly of animals. Black-and-white close-ups of birds, of an orangutan mother with the sweet ache of soul in her eyes. The oil paintings behind Chloe still worked their chemistry on her while she took in these photos, so different. The photographer had written testimony next to some of the images, telling where she had been and when.

Chloe knew the names of some of the places, but not all. How did the photographer find these moments that must have passed before she understood them? How did she go to all those different countries?

Chloe held her phone, wanting to say something to Daphnis, wanting to sketch or dance or cry. On one side human fantasies and the other animal truths, and together all these images overwhelmed her, made her feel young in a world that was long ago too old.

Daphnis dropped off bags at Harbour Pizza, each marked with letters for different customers. The delivery guys put the bags in the boxes with the pizza. They called Daphnis Red because of the colour of his bike and helmet. No one knew his face.

He didn't think about the bike and helmet making him conspicuous, that if someone wanted to tip off the police to distract them from other of the gang's concerns he would only have to say, "Follow the kid on the red motorbike."

Daphnis went to Harbour Pizza one day to make a drop and there were cop cars outside it, the deliverymen being led away in handcuffs.

He looked around and saw a cop staring at him from behind the wheel of his cruiser. The cop raised his hand from the wheel, staring hard at Daphnis, and made the sign of a gun.

How can you open your eyes to the world in search of beauty and not see its hazards and cruelty?

Over all these months Chloe was aware of the stare of Shane Dorcon, of the other bikers who now made the garage such a busy and threatening place.

Some days she could feel so confident and on others, for whatever reason, she was scared or pissed off, walking down the street, always watched, always a pack of yellow-eyed dogs waiting for the slightest shift of wind.

She handled their jokes and whistles and knew what to reach for in every part of the garage should any of them stand too close.

Maybe it was as simple as the season changing, cold nights creeping under doorways. Normally Chloe would spend a Saturday with Daphnis, but he was out doing something to make money. She wasn't sure what to do today. Sleep in. Some kind of worry keeping her awake.

Charlie took the bus with her to the garage and she hung out in her van, still a place where she felt free, despite the noise outside it. Saturdays weren't so busy. Charlie did a little work in the office and turned out a few lights, knocked on Chloe's door, but she had fallen asleep.

She woke up late in the afternoon feeling worse than she had in the morning. Usual sound of a tool dropping on the floor outside her van.

Her dad had sent a text saying *You were asleep went home.*

She checked the lock on the van's sliding door and sat on her bed, her back against the wall beneath the poster she had bought with Daphnis years before.

Where are you? she texted. *I'm scared.*

Daphnis stared back at the cop, looked at the road ahead. One of the Harbour Pizza guys was kneeling on the sidewalk, handcuffed. Daphnis knew this cop would chase him, one way or another, those knuckles were white on the steering wheel.

He revved the Super Hawk and wrote a letter *S* on the road, weaving around the noses of two cop cars, who fired their lights and chased him.

He saw a red light and the bike and helmet merged with it, Daphnis now a ray of light shooting hot and forward.

He brought the bike up to 120 and opened distance between himself and the cops. Stares and shouts from downtown pedestrians and then out to the purlieus where tires were stacked and the city dumped its dirt.

The police called for a third car, which tried to head him off at the entrance to Highway 1 but it didn't get there in time.

The bike responded to his hips and did what it was meant to do, the pair of them wild and nimble like a dog unleashed. The third car tried to make ground, but Daphnis could weave through traffic on the highway while the car had to wait for it to part.

There was one police helicopter in the city and it was summoned.

Daphnis took the exit to the River Road and the police cars didn't see him.

The hills started rising.

Only now did his mind catch up. *What are you doing, where are you going, how did the cops know? Slow down or you will die.* His mirrors told him the police weren't behind him, but he looked over his shoulder to confirm, gearing down and thinking.

No one knew what he looked like but for the helmet and bike. He had cash in his knapsack. He could find somewhere to hide the bike, call someone, get a cab, something.

He passed another scrapyard and thought he might leave the bike, but something made him twist the throttle and go towards the mountains. Running is easier than planning.

The helicopter rose over the city, south over Highway 1. It flew several miles beyond where the cruisers had last been close to the bike and then circled back. The River Road was the only obvious alternative to the highway.

This land, with its massive cedars. From above you could see that giants must have used it for harvest. The trees were thick near the roadside, but beyond the view of people on the ground were acres bald and torn where logging had happened for decades.

Protesters mounted jack-o'-lanterns along the roads used by loggers, their very faces becoming like jack-o'-lanterns themselves. Protesters setting fire to heavy equipment, the loggers beating them up in their encampments, all the enmity and curses, and none of them acknowledging that the greatest curse was that we will seldom know ourselves, seldom understand that our plastic and steel, from animal need, are as natural as the hills, and that we will kill and cry over what we kill.

Daphnis slowed the bike down. He turned down a logging road under the cover of trees and waited.

The helicopter passed, invisible, and made a ten-minute loop before heading back towards the city. With his engine off, his helmet off, Daphnis listened to the soughing of the breeze and had a sudden feeling that there were unimaginable mysteries remaining in these woods, stories of darkness and light.

He felt that if he went farther down that road into the woods he might be lost forever, and part of him wanted that.

He breathed in and took off his knapsack and looked at his phone. No cell service. His helmet was hanging on the handlebars. He stared into the woods and laid the bike down, leaving the key in it. Maybe there was someone living down that road like him whose dream would come true when he found the bike. He took his jacket off, put it in his knapsack, and walked back to the River Road.

In a logging truck on the way back to the city in the dark, Daphnis heard the story of the driver, a physician once who thought he understood the world, could even control it, until he drank it all away. Family, house, career. "These are the heaviest trucks I've driven," he said. Wanted to explain to Daphnis that he wasn't turning away from sadness but trying to drive into it as hard as he could.

Daphnis saw the message from Chloe on his phone, sent to him three hours earlier.

Scared.

BOOK THREE

I have been alive for so long and seen so many things. I saw the world before daylight, even before darkness as you may know it. Night was nothing like the lacquered thing you know, it was the first-born of Chaos and I simply can't breathe when I remember it, how we felt we were always falling.

The handful of us said prayers, and my job was to make everyone weak and unclever, make Night fall in love with Erebos and daylight come as their offspring.

Come the hills, come the rivers, come the milk spilled over the stars.

As much as I have seen, I think of it all as a fairly simple story. Strangers feel lonely in the woods; I, Love, help them meet each other. I make them hear music where there is none. I try to make them feel as much love for each other as I feel for them, and I often get it wrong.

Look at this landscape of unfinished houses. Couples who made plans and the money never came, some of them back in their parents' basement, back in the woods alone.

Look at this place I work in. An old folks' home where children leave their burdensome fathers. Perhaps I am needed here more than elsewhere.

These days I catch myself in the mirror, dressed as an orderly, moving from activity to activity, trying to make us all lively in the face of death. I suppose only the costume has changed.

I have asked this couple, the blind old man and his silent wife, "What did your house look like?"

And they have told me various things in their own way. They had a couple of houses. She loved the magnolia tree in front of one of them. He said he wanted to knock down walls to make that house feel bigger and I knew—he didn't need to tell me—that he had been going through a hard time in those days.

Some of the children who leave their parents here are elderly themselves. Many of them are kind, but I see the thoughts behind their smiles. *Is this how it will end?*

All our struggle. Everything I work for.

These children get angry at me sometimes and say, "My dad would never have wanted this."

I try to tell them that if you can love what you thought you never wanted, the world can feel rich, and huge. I try to tell them that these things they don't like the look of—these bleached corridors and hanging heads—all have a beautiful story behind them, of want and the not-quite-having. But if I told them I was responsible for all of that, they would get even angrier with me.

All the strange and ugly things in the world—if only I hadn't helped daylight come about, you say.

There is a story about the god Pan who was in love with a girl named Syrinx. Pan, of course, was part goat, part man, not very attractive to a young and beautiful girl. He promised her things and moved a little too close and she ran and hid among some reeds in a marsh far from home.

As Pan looked for her, she sank slowly into the marsh and disappeared.

Pan was angry and he cut down all the reeds, never finding the girl.

As time passed he felt guilty and understood that he had made Syrinx suffer, and he gathered the cut-down reeds in her honour.

He fashioned them in unequal lengths, because their love had been ill-matched, and bound them to make a pipe through which he played lovely music.

How many houses and songs are made from a love that is uneven.

How many girls have been lost.

Chloe didn't hear from Daphnis through the afternoon. She cautiously lifted a corner of one of her curtains in the van to see if Charlie might have come back.

The light in the office was off and Shane was busy at the far end of the shop, under a car with the radio on. As far as she could tell there was no one else around so she resolved to make her way home.

Winter was coming, the sun falling early. She heard another tool drop on the concrete, a curse, and she moved across the floor with purpose, touching the breast pocket of her coat where her phone was supposed to be.

It wasn't there, so she went back to her van and found it on the floor.

She didn't look towards Shane. Kept her head down.

He stepped out from behind a concrete pillar.

"Where are you going?" he asked.

She was startled.

The world had changed for Shane Dorcon.

He'd never lost his love for her. In fact, it had only grown. Her face and body, her innocence more complex. Elegant. Classy. Girl in the body of a woman. He tried to smell her whenever she passed and knew every line of her, every curve and journey from feet to hips to shoulders.

He looked at porn and dated other girls and none of it measured up.

On weekends he got into fights, thinking he might as well join the Jokers and forget about working for Mercedes. Milked money from Frank and got a hang of Coyote's game, distracted himself for stretches of time, but still there was this girl. He was on some kind of a swing where up near the sun was Chloe, he'd rush up and hope and never reach her. Down and back he would drop to the other place, the place of never having.

"Why don't you talk to me?"

"I'm just heading out," she said. She kept walking and turned to him so she wouldn't seem too rude. Moved backwards and hoped to reach the door.

"No, but I mean, you never talk to me these days. What's..." Her eyes made him nervous. What do you do when you dream of perfect eyes and there they are now staring back at you, all yours.

"Everyone's busy," she said, trying to smile. "I know you're working hard all the time."

"You see me?"

"Sure."

"Yeah, I've been saving. Working hard and saving cheese. You know. I've got plans."

"Awesome."

"I've learned a lot."

"Thing is, it's late," she said. "Mom and Dad get nervous when it's dark, you know."

"I can drive you home."

"No way. No, thanks... You're busy. Daphnis is going to call in a second and I'll walk and talk." She tried to keep her smile alive. "Thanks, Shane."

When she was turned it was like he had planned it, but he hadn't.

He grabbed a tire iron and swung at the side of her head and she collapsed like someone took her bones out.

Her face made a slapping sound when it hit the concrete.

Shane looked at her on the floor. How many times had he thought of knocking on the door of her van, just saying, "*Please*, can I come in," there was a bed back there and the fuckin van was red.

He wiped the tire iron with a shop cloth.

Crouched down and held his hand above her face. Dreamt so long of touching her but now he didn't want to.

He brought his car around to the back door and put her body in the trunk. Her blood was mostly in her hair, but he wiped the floor with the shop cloth and threw that in the trunk as well.

Back at his apartment, he took a couple of hits from his pipe. Couldn't remember what was in there, but hopefully it was calming. Next to his TV on the wall was a poster, a picture of the ocean that he used to like. Big waves, sun, the kind of place he thought he might end up at one day. Sometimes life can be about what you dream, not what you're living.

He picked up his phone and stared at it.

"I need your help," he said.

"Meet me at the clubhouse," said Coyote.

Even though that city was paradise to some, a place where deer wandered through gardens unmolested, it was also, to others, a bruised horizon of weathered billboards and empty parking lots. No future to it.

The last lumber mill in the city had closed ten years ago, and next to it sat the clubhouse of the Jokers, a place where the uninvited knew better than to visit but also a place that burned like a stove in a country cabin, a hot red glow of mistakes and strippers and a band of people saying fuck you to the lottery of birth.

The cops never went there. Everyone assumed it was either fear or a force of anti-magnetic like poles where the corruption of one met the corruption of the other and kept them apart.

Shane pulled up with Chloe's body in the trunk and Coyote met him outside.

"I killed her," he said. "I don't know what to do with it."

"Pull up around back."

Behind the clubhouse was the abandoned mill, and behind the clouds was the moon. It was hard to see anything. Certainly a distant stranger wouldn't have known what these men were doing, and it was hard enough to see inside the trunk.

Shane didn't want to look, and while he was turned and pacing, Coyote put his hand on her.

"I'll lift her. Leave her here and fuck off," said Coyote. "Get in the car."

Coyote lifted the body.

He said to Shane, "You owe me. Understand? If there's anything I want... Anything."

"I hear you. I hear you." He couldn't look at Coyote, and they both knew that kind of debt would be too much for Shane to handle.

He reversed the car, looking backwards. Drove away looking anywhere but at the man laying the body on the grass.

In the clubhouse, some of the men were sitting at the bar drinking and doing lines. The light was warm and golden and tigers hung mid-flight over the mind of every man, a brotherhood in the expectation of fights.

Bryan was sitting on the corner bench with some girls and Coyote said, "Come outside."

Shane decided not to go home. Something was sinking behind his eyes, some kind of truth. If the sun rises in the east you should always go west. He drove away hoping the darkness would never lift.

As Coyote walked down the hall to the back door with Bryan he said, "We need a doctor and some smack."

Daphnis was calling and texting Chloe, constantly, with *X*s and *O*s and that question several times now: *Where are you?* The phone in her breast pocket lighting up and vibrating over her heart.

Coyote took it out of her pocket and Bryan lifted her off the grass and carried her over his shoulder, upstairs to one of the rooms where the girls turned tricks. He injected her with a little brown for now to keep her out and he texted one of his junkie doctors who came and said he couldn't know anything without an X-ray but if it was a fractured skull it would be anywhere from a week to six months and who knew if there was brain damage.

They made her comfortable. Bryan gave her a little cocktail he'd been working on.

"Ease her into it," said Coyote.

Daphnis couldn't sleep that first night. He had gone to the garage twice, on his own and then with Charlie. Daphnis thought she must be mad at him for something, not spending enough time with her.

Nothing unusual inside the van.

Charlie called Shane, who had been in the garage that afternoon, but got no answer.

They called the police in the morning and filled out forms, neither Daphnis nor Charlie able to reduce her to facts about hair colour or size. "She's my daughter," said Sue.

In three weeks you could see Chloe there, on the missing persons website, Sue touching her face on the screen and asking, "How do they do it?"

The other parents whose kids had been missing for months and years.

That face kept Sue awake and she filled the moon with vodka.

The police went to Shane Dorcon's apartment and found nothing, traced his car and found him dead in the front seat, enough fentanyl to bring oblivion to the devil.

Every staple.

Look at all the staples on the wooden posts.

All the people missing. Families putting the staples in and praying or hoping. You're not giving up if you're pushing in a staple.

Most of those photos were rain-soaked and fading. Up on the light posts for as long as Daphnis could remember, meaning nothing to him before.

He went to her school.

To the rock by the lake.

Up and down her street in the cold, on his bike like when he was a kid.

Tried not to think or wonder.

Went to the garage and worked.

Coyote came with his car and said to Daphnis, "You shouldn't have gone to the cops. I can help you find her. We all can."

"How?"

"I know things. I know the cops are looking for a kid on a red bike who took them on a chase."

"I don't care."

"They'll be sniffing around."

"I don't care."

"Well. Meanwhile you owe me five grand for the bike. How're you gonna get that?"

"I don't know."

"Don't know, don't care, eh. Fix the car and we'll talk."

Black Lexus LC500.

Daphnis had to take out the back seat to get access to the fuel pump, the fuel lines in this model faulty.

Maroon cloth and leather for the boyfriends of a gangster.

There's a feeling in youth that you might never get there, to that solid place where wealth and certainty live, leather and comfort underpinning all endeavours. A feeling right now that nothing was worth anything.

As if he could read Daphnis's thoughts, Coyote said, "You've gotta earn it. Gotta fight. I fought for everything.

"Mother left me on the highway when I was five.

"What do you think of that?

"Six fuckin foster homes and I fought every day of my life. Knives and *teeth*."

He squeezed the headrest and summoned memories of the flesh he stabbed and acid he poured on the hands that held what he wanted.

Daphnis was taken out of his dull shock for a moment, felt like some great snake was rising behind him.

Coyote said nothing, but Daphnis felt it, a story or a warning from a landscape of half-eaten horses where predators killed for mischief not meat. A story about a reckoning and vengeance taken on a world run by middlemen and youth who have had it all given.

A snake is rising and watching.

"Gotta fight," said Coyote.

Sue's nights were blued by the TV screen.

Charlie got her pills and drew the curtains across her days and she had slurred conversations with Lina in her own blue room, two in the morning. Mothers dreaming. A whale swimming slowly in a vast wet house with the body of her baby attached.

"I saw it once," said Sue. "Whale swimming up and down. She had her dead baby for days because she was grieving and then let her go."

Lina listened.

"Milk full of plastic." Sue flicked the blister pack of some pills. "Mother's milk was poison and it killed the baby and she let the baby go. Sank to some place they couldn't film it."

At the clubhouse, Bryan's girlfriend Jenna put a new ad on Bedpage and Skip the Games.

New girl in town. One week only.

Bryan had given Chloe another dose and she was sleeping next to Jenna, who wrote *Angel* on her laptop.

New girl in town. One week only. Call or text: Angel.

Coyote grossed around $300,000 per girl per year, if each got fifteen to twenty clients a day.

Moved them to other cities, kept things fresh.

Jenna stroked Chloe's face and thought this is how it is, how it is.

Got some underwear for her and plastic ties.

The clerk at the Quality Inn had seen them come and go, some much younger than Chloe. He got a kickback once a month from the gang and the rooms were guaranteed to be rented by the week.

The first text came to Jenna's phone from a businessman named Fred who said he was flying in for three days. Probably not named Fred and possibly a cop.

A little banter from Jenna, who pretended to be Angel.

You're my first! she wrote.

Ha! wrote Fred. *First of the week?! This city?*

First ever, wrote Angel.

Sure! said Fred.

He always knew it could be a cop or some guy waiting to rob him.

Lemme see another pic! Take one now.

Jenna held the phone near Chloe's face and tried to find the best angle. Put the bedside clock in the frame to show the time.

Very sleepy, she wrote.

Wow! wrote Fred. *Beautiful.*

Keeping bed warm.

How old?

Eighteen! ;;;;

He texted later in the morning. *Meeting ran late. There at 11:30.*

Ok.

What room?

614. Come straight up, BB.

There was a timing with the new girls that Bryan and Jenna had perfected over the past couple of years, Bryan getting the dose right so they weren't out cold and Jenna getting the clients in while the girls were coasting. Once they were hooked, it didn't matter.

A woman larger and more hardened than the pictures was at the door when Fred knocked.

"Ah," he said.

"I'm Catherine," said Jenna, holding her pepper spray in her pocket.

Fred was a little bald man in his forties.

"Come in," she said. "She's on the bed. Cash up front."

Fred had prepared the money.

"Do you want me to cut them?" she asked.

"Um... Yes."

Jenna got her pocket knife and cut the ties from Chloe's wrists.

"Is she asleep?"

"Maybe. You'll wake her. I'll be back in half an hour."

When Jenna left, Fred took off his coat and stroked Chloe's face with the back of his fingers.

"Angel," he said.

They say that Love, like an angel, has wings.

Hummingbird.

Needle in nectar.

Cupid hovering outside that window, weeping.

Chloe was on a beach with Daphnis, so tired. Truly alone for the first time, no parents or mechanics or consciences saying don't, not yet, not here.

So tired.

This was that beach that everyone wanted to visit, the ocean *perfect,* the sun spilling golden promises on those who pray for peace, who pray for each other, please let this last forever.

And it didn't last.

As always, a teacher appeared with a mouth full of coffee and decay, and the teacher said, "You're mine. You're what I was and wanted to be.

"My Angel."

A knife from the underworld, between her legs, and a teacher licking her face, but Daphnis, her Daphnis, was that warm beach and the sun. "Everything's going to be great," he said.

And Cupid banged his face on the window, trying to get in.

Bryan had fucked up the dose sometimes. They'd had to take a few of the girls to the ravine. But he was a master, in Jenna's eyes. A way out of this shit one day. Much younger than her, but manly. Coyote's trusted guy who did a lot of dirty work but got paid well and knew how to hide his feelings about Coyote fucking boys.

Jenna and Bryan had bought their house with cash, and the dogs. Had the Harley and the Lincoln and the Jet Ski for the summer. Hunger and drugs killed Jenna's parents and they weren't going to get Jenna anymore. There were better ways to forget.

She came back in half an hour and, like most of the others who called themselves businessmen or gentlemen, Fred didn't look her in the eye when he left.

Jenna got a washcloth and cleaned up Chloe to be ready in half an hour for the next.

Chloe made noises and squirmed in a way that Jenna knew.

She texted Bryan. *Might need a little more over here.*

He came with his spoons and needles and Daphnis filled her body with gold.

A golden statue.

He entered as liquid, molten, and he took shape inside her as he cooled, a statue in exactly her form, her hero.

Bryan could judge them all by weight. Girls in bars. Even in layers of jackets and sweaters he knew how much it would take to make them his. An artist. Chloe was feeling exactly what he wanted her to feel.

Daphnis looked like Bryan. Daphnis looked like many men. When you find your true love he looks like everyone you've dreamt of, and you forget everyone you've dreamt of because there is only one true love. Daphnis cooked the gold in spoons.

Bryan and Jenna slept on the second bed in the hotel room. She sucked him off and dreamt and planned and Jenna brought Chloe strawberries and ice cream because the girls always loved sweet things.

Everyone loved sweet things. The lot surrounding the Quality Inn hosted every kind of man, handsome or ghastly or otherwise, all with something more than hunger wetting their mouths. Some of them alone since birth, some well-married but insatiable. A grey procession in winter rain, a haunting of the parking lot, the men walking slowly from their cars, a coach, adjuster, a dentist, looking no one in the eye. One day a welder cashed a cheque and did doughnuts in his Charger on the tarmac.

The strawberries were such an exquisite gift for Chloe.

She'd been in a jungle under constant attack from apes with clubs and hot swords, she'd never had a dream so scary.

Mom and Dad were screaming from a tower and they jumped to a golden lake or a rusty pond and died and Chloe floated above them looking at their sad and silent faces. She was disappointing them over, and over, and over, and felt so sad.

The apes were lined up all the way down the road, deep into the jungle, sometimes in front, sometimes behind, and when they were chasing her she got clear for a second, up ahead, *please just let me run,* and that's when the tree appeared, the one with all the berries.

A strawberry is the sweetest piece of the heart, the piece that makes a child love a parent.

Let's say a man does all kinds of wrong, and beats and shouts at his family, and is walking down the courthouse steps. His little child will wait for him and take his hand and will still look up to him because of the strawberry in her heart.

Daphnis and Charlie drove the streets at night together.

Not once did they mention aloud the possibility that she was gone, that Dorcon killed her and then killed himself.

Lina flinched whenever she heard a motorbike on the street, but she otherwise tried to stay strong for Sue. She and Frank tried to keep things running, Frank going into the garage more than usual.

All the bikers in their lives now, they had to be involved somehow.

Those entitled fucks with the SUVs bullying money out of the little people. There will, indeed, be a reckoning.

Daphnis clenched his fists in the shower in the morning but at night had dreams in the opposite spirit where there was no fight left in him, no hope.

Made his bed every morning because the more normal you make things the more likely they'll be normal, just the same. *It's a year ago,* he told himself. *The world is a year ago and it's fine.*

"I'll give you anything," he said to the sky.

Uncle Charlie had given Daphnis lots of advice over the years about how to be a good mechanic.

"It takes courage to fix something yourself, instead of paying someone to do it. It's not about money. You need courage, you need patience. You need to learn how to do things. Creativity. And you need a tool. Anything that's built can be taken apart, and anything can be built if you've got the right spirit and a tool."

Daphnis didn't tell Charlie about working at the dial-a-dope or that he owed Coyote five grand. He grew more silent.

There was a way to fix all of this, he knew it. He just needed a tool.

Girls Chloe's age waited at bus stops. They hung around malls and walked out of bars in shoes they weren't used to. The pulse of Charlie and Daphnis quickened if a girl like that appeared under a street light and Charlie felt an old flash of guilt for his desires, sick for wanting beauty.

They sighed and quietly strengthened each other's resolve.

Lina held Sue's hand when seven weeks had passed and said, "Have faith." Tried to get Sue out of her bedroom and walking. Sat outside under blankets in Lina's garden and said, "Sometimes I forget there's birds in winter."

"I never asked for her," said Sue. "I hoped. But I never expected."

"I know."

"Part of me expected this. Losing her."

Lina looked at the birds.

"Things were too good," said Sue.

Daphnis felt Chloe alive in the air, in whispers, in the sound of soaked city streets.

"I love you," she said.

"I love you," said Daphnis.

"I love you," said Chloe to Bryan.

"You love what I'm giving you," said Bryan.

It didn't matter anymore, keeping them doped.

The less he drugged them now, the more they would do.

The pain of everything became unbearable to Chloe. Her body, her injuries, her present days and memories. Throwing up through moments of lucidity. She looked around some of the rooms they kept her in, recognized Bryan from the garage and held her arm out to him hopefully, did whatever he said, saw jeans on a chair that she thought she used to wear, and tried to sit up with her back straight but her torso fell forward, and she travelled into the bedspread across her legs, not feeling her legs until the pain came back and she held out her arm for Bryan. The only thing that ever helped was Daphnis in the needles.

Jenna arranged a train of men, twelve guys at once, five grand for two hours of work, dull slap of skin, of meat thrown in bins by a butcher, and the train dragging slowly to every stop.

"Just kill me," said Chloe to Bryan.

"We'll kill your family," said Jenna. "Understand? Tell everyone you're a hoor and kill your fuckin family."

They brought her to the clubhouse for a few days during her time of the month and raised her dose. Walls and ceiling painted black and Chloe told herself the weather was going to change, pulled at the door to make the weather change.

In her family home, Sue took clonazepam and maybe they met on the same green cloud.

Jenna brought Chloe strawberries sometimes and said, "You'll like this life. Deep down. You will, the older you get. All the attention. We've all done it. There's good coin in dancing. Travel the country. I saw the big waterfall there, and all the big cities."

In South End the smokestacks whistled with smells of rust and chlorine. Coyote had a house on the water, a treadmill set up by a big window where he walked as if he was travelling over the strait.

"You'll work for me," he said to Daphnis, who stood silent beside the treadmill. "With those fists. That clean face, they'll never see it coming. Out there behind us is a city full of bums who owe me money. Street dealers."

Daphnis looked around the room. A guy his age in a buttoned-down shirt sat on a couch at the far wall, raising his face occasionally from his phone to look at the view, at Coyote on the treadmill, at Daphnis.

Coyote looked at him and Daphnis. "He thinks you're gonna replace him," he said. "You're making him worried."

Coyote liked to challenge his young friends, wanted to shape them all, see if they could handle even half of what he had endured. Watch them walk through fire and grow beholden to him.

"You'll get a piece of whatever you collect. Fighter like you can do it without a gun."

Daphnis went to the apartments of dealers who were meant to be kicking up regularly to Coyote. Some were habitually late, junkies themselves, and they all had names like Cougar and Brick that gave away nothing about their nature. There was a surprise behind every door and relief in being angry. Relief in not believing that Chloe was gone and life had no purpose or meaning.

He tried to remember everything his coach had taught him, but instead of fighting with love in his heart he fought for it, as if his fists were tools for clearing away weeds, knocking down trees that stood in the way of Love's altar. Chloe was being held somewhere and he had to make a path.

He taped his fists before he opened doors.

To some of the dealers it seemed funny that this was the person Coyote had sent as muscle, and they found themselves lying on the floor during his visit trying to remember what they had found amusing. Some of them had knives and one had a girlfriend high on meth who saw in Daphnis everything she had lost from youth, the boys she'd loved, the prayers she had held up to the sky that hated the sight of her. The drug made her manic and fearless and she attacked the head and back of Daphnis while he tried to get money from her boyfriend. A terrible force in that room that could have united them all, Daphnis, the dealer, and the girlfriend, three solitudes who wanted nothing more than to see better days.

Word got back to Coyote that Daphnis was good at his job, and Daphnis, of course, brought him money. He got close to earning the five thousand he owed Coyote for the bike but still nowhere near being able to help with his dad's debt.

Coyote had a dream about Daphnis, that he rose from the water as a lambent god and made Coyote his supplicant. Humiliated him with his beauty.

"You make me feel young," he said to a boy named Brad he picked up at the Shepherds. Touching his face as gently as he could.

Brad said filthy things and Coyote put a hand on his face, squeezed his cheeks together so his lips looked ridiculous, and said, "You look stupid when you talk dirty."

He went through a boy every month.

Coyote invited Daphnis to the clubhouse and sat him at the bar, a kind of giddiness in his heart as he knew that night that Chloe lay in a bed upstairs, and he stared at the face of Daphnis, the beautiful god from his dream. *I'll cut you into ribbons,* he thought.

"Any word about that girl of yours?"

"No."

"Are you talking to the cops?"

"They're no help."

"Well, they make websites. Everyone puts things on websites and thinks they're doing work. Drink up."

A shot of bourbon sat untouched in front of Daphnis.

"I need the bathroom."

Coyote gestured at Bryan behind the bar, who put a little pill in the shot, for sport, once Daphnis disappeared.

"You sure it's smart to have him sniffing around here?"

"You're asking me two things," said Coyote. "If I'm sure or if I'm smart."

"No, I'm—"

"You tell me which is smarter—keeping your eye on a snake or turning your back to it."

Coyote stared at Bryan, having kept his eye on him for ten years.

"You got that girl ready for touring yet?"

"Pretty much."

"Then do it. I don't want to feed her anymore."

Coyote looked over at Brad on the corner bench, who crossed his legs and smiled back.

The clubhouse walls were hung with patches and jackets, newspaper articles about biker wars and drug deals, a couple of old rifles and framed porn posters, Head Nurse and All in One.

The windows were boarded over and drum and bass played. Thursdays were the parties when heroin and coke were laid in mounds like spices at a bazaar and girls with menacing eyes licked tequila off their fingers and the bartop.

"Drink," said Coyote to Daphnis.

"Drink your fuckin drink," said Bryan.

"Anything you want is yours," said Coyote, gesturing around. "Game of pool. Little coke. I know you don't want girls. Smart guys don't need girls."

"You have any idea what I had to do for my patch?" said Bryan.

"Bryan's gonna get jealous," said Coyote. He put his hand on Daphnis's back. "Don't rise too fast. And don't get old," he said, smiling.

"Drink," said Bryan.

They loomed over Daphnis, and a girl named Lucy who wore a string bikini swung a cloth-covered ceiling lamp towards the bar, back and forth on its long wire, saying, "Play with me," each time she caught it.

"Don't ignore Lucy," said Coyote, and Daphnis turned around.

Lucy held the lamp up to his face.

"You're pretty," she said.

A boy, thought Coyote. How was he still a boy. He ran through scenarios quickly, Lucy having let the light swing back, swooning visions in Coyote's mind of holding a gun to the head of Daphnis while Lucy made the boy burst with her mouth.

Coyote looked to Bryan and gestured.

"Drink!" said Bryan. "I want to show you something."

Bryan took Daphnis to the office, a room behind the bar where a TV on the wall showed loops of naked women fighting. Daphnis was wise to feeling fucked-up around Bryan and he tried to hold steady. The women on the screen were pulling hair and slapping each other red.

Daphnis watched Bryan put on a pair of blue latex gloves and retrieve something from a drawer in the desk.

"Check this out," he said. "A Mauser C96. Broomhandle gun."

He handed a long-barrelled pistol to Daphnis, who held it and stared.

"Antique," said Bryan.

Daphnis tried to focus on this odd-looking thing, squared chamber in front of the trigger and a wooden handle with a red number nine carved into it.

"Semi-automatic. Seven bullets. You can use that one day. Boss wanted me to show you. Catch whoever took your girl."

Daphnis stared and thought and weighed it.

A tool.

Bryan put a Jokers ball cap on Daphnis, pulled down the peak.

"Cute," he said.

Took off the cap and laid it and the gun on the desk.

Daphnis was suddenly back out in the bar and chunks of the night went missing.

"You've got a big job coming up," said Coyote. "Collect from a fat, rich fuck we call the Dolphin. Bigger money now, golden boy. Higher stakes. He cleans money for us and he owes me some. Lots."

He held the golden face in his hand.

"Keep your focus. Keep your mind clean," he said.

Daphnis thought about the gun in the morning.

Bryan and his gloves.

There are times in life when we squarely occupy our bodies, when fictions are revealed and either sloughed or consciously embraced. Those who do it honestly realize they are alone, that their works and sadness are of equal inconsequence and their lives will be footprints in snow.

But they run still, and build, and they work nonetheless because there is no beauty in cowering.

Life may otherwise amount to a hallway of darkened length in an infinite motel where satyrs come and go through doorways to writhe and drool over the failure of their dreams. Dirty fingernails. Hollow and obscene declarations.

A gong of salvation after every pill or needle and fear of agony between.

Jenna told Chloe bedtime stories, tales of her own life, how she, too, was once in love with a boy who looked like Daphnis, not the practical and respectful love she felt for Bryan but the kind Chloe knew that gave a rose its colour and thorns. And she had a baby with this love, a boy she left behind because she, like Chloe, was hooked.

"Someone's coming," said Chloe. "Someone. To pick me up."

Jenna put her thumb beside Chloe's lips to wipe the drool.

"If only someone came and saved me," said Jenna. "That's what I used to think. If someone came and saved me." She pulled up her belt so it sat higher on her belly. "You can only save yourself."

They planned to take Chloe across the water to the mainland and tour her through the bigger cities, make her truly new in town. One week only. Such a beautiful girl that she had repeat customers. When she was high she could twist and hiss like a snake now, a cat, a minx, or a lynx or whatever the fuck they wanted. She could look down at her body from above and laugh at how she fooled them.

Jenna stood outside the door sometimes and smoked. Made sure that Chloe didn't run away and Chloe tried over and over, barely aware of what she was thinking but knowing she had to run. Her body weaker each time, and Jenna sucking questions through her smoke. She got drunk and kept a mini of vodka in her bag for nerves and started wondering if she should just let her go, let go of all their plans.

Jenna could go weeks sometimes not knowing she was drunk until she got sober again, sometimes forgot what happened in a day and wondered what was real. People appeared to her and then vanished.

One day a client made arrangements to meet and he disarmed Jenna at the door. A face she could love. A charm that seldom existed in the realm of money and sex. He wore a handsome suit and the suit was the colour of a bruise.

His face, habitually happy, seemed melancholy, and Jenna wished to comfort him.

"I'll be back in half an hour," she said, but he held out a hand almost touching her.

"No," he said. "You stay."

He led her towards Chloe's bed and Jenna said, "No, I don't... I shouldn't," and he smiled and said, "Sit there, please."

Jenna sat on the spare bed and the young man sat at the edge of Chloe's. Jenna had left the door open.

At this point Chloe would normally unzip her body, climb to the ceiling with scorn, or look out the window at plastic bags in trees. But the young man used a gentle thumb to pull some strands of hair out of her eyes. He touched her forehead like no one had for weeks and said, "I know you."

Jenna got nervous and felt for the phone and mace in her bag. But she also saw herself on the bed, it was her fingers touching that face and the handsome man wasn't there.

"I've read about you," he said to Chloe. "For thousands of years."

The room was quiet except for the tick of the cheap clock by the bed and traffic sounds outside.

"Some people suffer so much," he said. His voice was Jenna's. "So much more than others. And I try to write it down. I have pens made from sharpened feathers and I write on people's hearts. But this..." He looked around at the stains and broken souls and what he had seen through the windows. Knew that Jenna wanted to love.

"I've seen a man shoot his wife in the head, and then himself. I've seen it in office buildings and streetside bars. Children burned with cigarettes and mothers unmanning their sons. All these people hating each other for the love of something higher. For love, they say.

"I've had many imposters."

He shifted and Chloe's fingers touched Jenna's leg.

"The stars and planets aren't stars and planets," he said. "They're the heroes who made it through. I think about all the ships that need their light."

What a face he had. Leaning closer with a sad and hopeful smile.

He stood up and walked out without looking at Jenna, without closing the door.

Jenna rose and watched him. Sat again at the end of the bed still staring at the open door and the daylight coming in.

Chloe looked at Jenna's back and slowly got out of bed. Her jeans were loose when she pulled them on and she was dizzy. Could only just remember how to tie her laces, and the act of getting dressed seemed perverse when what she wanted was to find the rain and wash her skin right off.

She held on to the dresser and looked towards the door, Jenna still saying nothing.

Jenna watching the girl pass by, cloudy outside, the day night's only cure.

BOOK FOUR

Twenty-three years before that day, a local boy named Danny was trying to be a photographer. He saw things that others couldn't, a poetry to the body, man or woman, that could only be expressed through taking pictures—these marks on a page inadequate to him for describing the glory of flesh.

He wanted his photos to hang in galleries, like Mapplethorpe's or Newton's, landscapes of skin that would titillate and make people look within.

"You're naked under your clothes," was something he liked to say to lovers; an obvious fact, of course, but surprising to him in relation to all the seekers and all the pundits making pronouncements about who we are. Danny believed that if you want to understand people, don't look at the outfit, look at the animal.

He was beautiful. Perhaps one reason he enjoyed nudity as much as he did was that he loved seeing the effects he had on people he lay down with. Almost indiscriminate in the lovers he took—middle-aged clerks, young waitresses, bus drivers—not because he didn't need beauty but because he loved how they responded to his. The great undoing. The collapse of their defences.

He believed in universal error, the flaws that unite us all, and he wanted to milk that error from everyone. As much as Danny was admired, he ended relationships badly, taking his yearning for honesty as far as it would go and often leaving friendships and marriages ruined.

One night he met a man his age named Raymond at a bar frequented by artists. There was clarity in Raymond's eyes and an aura around him that was different from other artists. It turned out that Raymond wasn't an artist at all, he was a thief who was casing the bar.

"You have a cruel smile," said Danny, and it was the beginning of a deep and painful love.

Raymond was strong, a wiry twenty-nine-year-old who had had a hard life. Stories from it emerged over time, in and out of prison, drawn to crime first out of need and then through making a success of it.

At bars he and Danny played games, competed for the attention of men and women, and the men and women were always drawn to Danny. He and Raymond would go home together and Raymond would punish him, act the role of jealous lover, be the jealous lover. He broke Danny's jaw and beat him with belts and they both did a lot of cocaine.

Always regret in the morning or when the flame of coke subsided, a heavy darkness in both as they felt for different reasons that the world did not have a place for them.

"If I don't get clean," said Raymond, "I'm gonna end up back there."

Danny had his head on Raymond's chest, caressing the tattoos he'd got in prison. Danny stood up naked, shoulders like golden apples on a golden tree.

"Where should I get a tattoo?"

Raymond took in the sight of him. "Don't ruin that," he said.

Danny looked at himself in a full-length mirror. An art school friend had told him myths about Narcissus, an obscure sequence he painted where another man was in love with the beautiful boy and the boy told that man to kill himself. Even gave him a sword.

"Narcissus was cursed to love himself by a man he didn't love."

"I don't need your love," said Raymond.

A pattern began that day, where every time Danny wanted a tattoo Raymond would get one as proxy. "Stay beautiful," he always said, at first with a kind of yearning and later as a command.

Some lovers are perfectly wrong for each other. Danny kind, Raymond cruel, Danny high, Raymond clean and sober. The more Danny partied, the worse Raymond looked, as if all the former's corruption was being embodied by the other and written in tattoos.

Raymond was in with the local bikers and was rising in the ranks. His sobriety became a strength. He felt more powerful the more he resisted booze and drugs.

He found himself inflamed by Danny's beauty, more needy of it, perhaps, the same constant comfort and temptation that he felt near drugs. One day he might give in and get high or cut Danny's throat before he lost his looks.

"You like hurting me," said Danny.

"I do."

The more Raymond abused him, the more Danny felt he was looking down life's dark hallways—a kind of ambassador for those who were less courageous, wishing his photos could bear witness to the things he saw.

His search for error began in a compassionate and curious place, but the older he got, and the higher, the more that search became the opposite of love, the shadow of it. Raymond was more full of error than anyone Danny knew and he doled out gentle torture in keeping his business with the bikers a secret from him. How many friends and strangers he had killed. Secrets as compelling to Danny as wealth and achievements might be to other lovers.

When things were ugly, when Raymond had a chance to say, "You're the only thing I think of, you're what I see when I do these things," he didn't. And he didn't because that was never what he felt. Things had always been ugly and always would be for Raymond, he'd been lost since he was a boy.

They went for longer stretches without seeing each other and their reunions became more passionate, more violent. The shine of Danny's youth was fading quickly because of the drink and drugs. "You're too afraid to hurt me properly," he said, dragging the end of his belt across Raymond's face and taunting him. He would laugh when Raymond hit him, and he had to go to the hospital a couple of times.

For a while his life went in two directions, the hallways he travelled with Raymond and a search for some kind of brighter beauty elsewhere, an antidote. He found models, all kinds of women who succumbed to his charms, who partied with him and posed.

He wasn't sober enough to see that his photos didn't find the rapture both he and the women longed for. Smiles without light behind them. Bruises. A smear of dirt on a print and legs spread out of a wish to desire rather than from desire itself. If there was art to the images or if the bruises spoke of vulnerability and survival, they might have climbed a gallery wall, but they mostly spoke of Danny losing his potential.

There was one woman, though, who loved him beyond control. She was thirty-five and in a marriage whose fire had gone dark, who didn't realize how desperately she had wanted new life until she met Danny at a gallery downtown. She said the veins on his arms were like lightning.

Danny loved her, in his way. If he made her feel love, made her think that she had never been so alive and that money and possessions were simply counterfeit and pretenders to this true royalty, then he fulfilled a noble purpose. There might not be a more splendid gift than to make someone feel love.

And she was, in fact, quite wealthy. She bought Danny camera equipment and a van. Treated him to dinners, discreetly. That little bit older, enough for her to be maternal sometimes. She knew he had other lovers and was sometimes jealous, but her love was so great that if she knew he would be happy floating away with twenty other women, she would blow kind breath at the sail.

When you feel pure love, she realized, you attain the highest wisdom. Life becomes very simple. Each day's purpose is clear: love.

It made her radiant. Her husband felt breathless with her anew, her green eyes and smile that had long before been his medicine. "I've always loved you," he said. "Life gets too noisy and I forget."

"You don't forget love," she said.

She thought of Danny when she was in bed with her husband, tried to summon him, but it made her miserable. She understood for the first time how one's body was sometimes not one's own.

She got pregnant, and wondered if it was Danny's, and the ownership of her body took on new dimensions. A seedbed for love, a factory of promise, her body could nourish a miracle.

Danny got high and kept chasing, running both paths and finding Raymond's had no end.

He put a bed in the back of his van and visited Raymond, who held a straight razor to Danny's neck while they made love.

"Cut pieces off me," said Danny. "I want to feel."

"No."

"Do it. I'll tell them you're weak. I'll go to your fuckin clubhouse and tell them."

He was skinny now, all the more flimsy in Raymond's arms. Raymond watched him get high and flail around the room naked, hissing about strange visions and gods who would do his bidding if he brought gifts of burning wine.

"You're a piece of shit," said Raymond.

It seemed the end now for Danny. No fame, no career, his ability to excite the love and honesty of strangers no more. He cried and Raymond held him. A power Raymond felt for the next twenty years, the dealer's over the junkie. But that body he controlled still held some kind of sway.

"Your smile is getting crueller," said Danny. "It's more convincing." He pinched a tattoo on Raymond's arm. "You should get one on your face. On your ears. Tattoo your fuckin ears and see if your smile still works."

Danny hung his favourite photos in his van and lived in it.

She recognized the light-blue van one day as she was driving to pick up her baby from her mother's, and she pulled over and parked in front of it.

Those early days she wondered all the time whether the baby was Danny's. Searched that miraculous face, that world, and looked for signs and memories, little veins too hidden to reveal their lightning.

She looked in her rear-view and saw Danny, haggard and asleep behind the wheel. Still the face of her lover, on a different journey now.

"I have a daughter," she said, as if Danny were in the car with her.

She drove away, but it wasn't the last she saw of him.

He smoked a few pipes and drank and the mischief popped and hissed and the sadness kept threatening to kill him. Light a sweet blue fire up ahead and rest on a sea of vodka. He had no money for tomorrow, that was the thing.

That's what made him go to her house.

He had memories of that place. Always fun to fuck people in the middle of their lives, to know the real truth, the one their partners didn't. Nice place, money, pretty girl. Beautiful, in fact. Never got photos of her. What happened to those days?

Her hips against his and that look in her eyes. Real love.

He lit another pipe and thought about money. That light in her eyes from the fire of love, that was the light shining through the windows now, mist of gold in the night.

Money.

He took a deeper hit, a little too deep, and he was moving now at the mercy of the master. Floppy puppet. He was a floppy puppet on the strings of Raymond, Raymond could get him more hits.

He didn't remember much in the morning. The search for gold. Anything gold. If she could get that light in her eyes back. It was like she didn't know who he was. Husband not home, old times' sake.

"She's not our daughter, she's mine," she said.

He remembered stabbing her in the belly because he had never done that, and he remembered the search for gold.

In the van in the morning, nothing in his pockets, no drugs, no cash. A pair of gold shoes, a belt, and a screaming baby.

Danny had never known such pain. The agony of not being able to die.

There were layers of clarity and confusion in his head through the day. Clarity about his need for more crack, the places he might get it. Confusion about whether this was real.

He wrote a note and parked the van outside a garage and felt a brief relief to close the door on it.

The pain controlled him all day, not able to score anywhere, and the clarity guided him as night fell to the clubhouse of the Jokers.

Raymond saw him come in before anyone else did. He was sitting at the bar and got up, walked towards the junkie.

Danny saw his love coming closer with tattooed ears and the smile that still worked, feeling happy that he could yet make Raymond like the look of him.

And Raymond swiped the razor across his throat before he could speak, a blood offering like a cock, a goose, or a lamb to the table of gods who feigned indifference but rained caprice, injustice, and glory on that island every day.

And if there were a ledger of all your prayers, perhaps there would be fewer sacrifices, the balance not in favour of hope; but every time this story has been told it reaches me as a prayer I can't deny. The story where Cupid, the god of Love, looks over a girl who loves; where the girl with shrinking cause to love is reunited with a boy who would never be whole without her.

At the clubhouse bar that night years ago, in the corner, was a prospect named George Nathon, who from a young age was adept at spotting fellow liars. Like Coyote, he could stand in a bar and pick out every addict, exploit the weakness of everyone he met. He watched Raymond walk towards Danny and cut his throat, and he held a flip phone that caught five grainy photos of the act.

He helped Raymond clean up the mess and he recorded all interactions, quickly gathering all kinds of material to hold sway over Raymond for decades.

Nathon was not only a prospect, he was a cop.

For almost twenty years Raymond, known as Coyote, was an informant for the police, tipping off Nathon on deals and hits, sharing knowledge of every member of his gang and many of his rivals. Coyote made a show of kicking Nathon out of the Jokers and he seemed to disappear from their orbit. But over those years they played each other, back scratches and threats, until Coyote and the Jokers became the most powerful gang on the island and George Nathon got rich.

The Dolphin. White-collar criminal of the sea. Nathon had a preoccupation with cameras, listening devices, computers, and had always been good with numbers. He learned as he locked people up and recorded their secrets that the world was not owned by those who made things or who built important businesses but by the ones who controlled their money. And he got wise early to the strength he could wield by having the latest technology—how strong are the ones behind the light, watching the world go blind.

He left the police and laundered money for the gangs. Set up small businesses, used the casinos and crypto, and most of all engaged in the diamond trade, using rough diamonds to clean Coyote's money. Investments brought him wealth, and cameras gathered all kinds of information to use for leverage. His hunger increased the more he ate, and folds crept up the back of his bald head, and he earned himself the nickname the Dolphin, plump and smooth and smart.

Coyote never forgot that the Dolphin had taken those five grainy photos. He was the one person left in the city who ever had anything over him.

When Daphnis went to the Dolphin's house in the morning, a mist hung over the island, a frequent mist that catered to thieves and surprises.

He had taped his knuckles and he stood outside the house, trying to figure things out. To that point he had collected from small dealers, businesses, people in messy apartments. This place, high on the mountain, belonged to someone closer to the gods.

How was he meant to scare a man who lived in a house like this?

The door was on the side built into rock, this part of the house clad in corten steel, the whole thing crouching as if to hide its wealth. The steel of the door itself must have weighed a thousand pounds, hinges making it weightless, and it was open a few inches.

Best fighter sees it all, said Daphnis to himself. Stepping lightly, under the camera at the doorway.

He walked towards windows, floor to ceiling, at the far end of that level. Looked around at the open space, the whole house oriented towards that view: the city and ocean where the mist had not yet settled and two golden eagles wheeled at a height below the house.

The sky was reflected on a polished concrete floor, and the huge open space was furnished with art and sparse and simple objects unreckonable to a boy who grew up in a garage. A wall of white oak slats had been torn open as if by a bear, some of the slats lying on the floor and others fanned out from the base. The drywall behind was pulled off and several stud cavities exposed.

The world has always been peopled by masters, middlemen, and slaves, the last seldom entering a space like this except to serve. Daphnis didn't know where to look, but it was clear that someone had recently been here looking for treasure in the walls. In one of the cavities was an empty paper bill strap reading *$10,000*. A cracked battery cover and a pry bar that had likely done the damage to the walls.

He looked around, over his shoulder. Light from the window glinted off liquid on the counter across the room, and there on the floor behind the kitchen island was a bald, blueing corpse in a housecoat, like his namesake washed up on a beach.

The Dolphin was lying face down, a bullet hole in the back of his large head and two in the back of his housecoat. And there at the body's feet were a gun and a hat, the hat a Jokers ball cap and the gun a long-barrelled pistol with a red number nine on the handle.

The police had kept their cars silent. Six of them were surrounding the house and if it hadn't been for the chirp of a two-way radio, Daphnis would not have heard their approach. One was through the front door, the others were below the windows and waiting outside the garage one storey below.

Daphnis realized when he heard the chirp that he had been framed. The gun with his prints on it, his hair in the hat.

He tried to move quietly. Grabbed the gun and the hat and found a door that led to a pantry behind the kitchen.

The Dolphin once told Coyote that the difference between chaos and dancing was music.

"You can look at a room full of people and they'll all be doing their own thing, talking, fighting, what have you. But if you play the right music in that room, most of them will dance."

His point was that whoever played the music had the power.

Coyote was driving his Lexus across town playing Mahler's Fifth, the Adagietto that Danny had played for him on a rare calm morning, harp pulling pizzicato plums from a sad and creamy sky. He could picture the dance from above, a slow one.

Jenna had called Bryan and said she couldn't run the girls anymore. Said she had let the girl from the garage walk away. And Coyote told Bryan that they had all sworn a vow, something bigger than themselves, and if you didn't honour that thing, everything else would fall apart.

"If you can sell girls, you can buy them," he said, which Bryan took to mean that Jenna could be replaced.

After so many years of dealing with Nathon, Coyote knew that everything in his life was wired; his house a fortress; his very body a vehicle for surveillance. But as wise and controlling as the Dolphin was, his world had a simple weakness.

He and Bryan went to Nathon's house at 4 a.m., Duane from the electric company killing his line and Bryan taking an axe to the conduit from the generator. Without electricity, Nathon had nothing.

Coyote wanted the body more or less fresh for the cops and Daphnis to find that morning. His old friend George whom he had hated for decades. No neighbours to hear the three thunderous shots from the Mauser.

Bryan tore the wall off and found the cash and papers and the phone, but no diamonds. There should have been hundreds of rough stones.

The dance going wrong for Coyote.

With the Mahler in his head, he went to his window at home, stared out at the sea. The same two golden eagles that Daphnis watched from above were circling, trying to decide which innocents to remove from earth.

The pantry at the Dolphin's was twenty feet deep and at the far end was another door. No light to guide him. Daphnis opened the door and smelled tires, machinery, tried to see where he was. The security door pushed against his back. He put the gun and hat down and fumbled for his phone, light flashing over a large garage and he was standing over steps leading down to it. He leaned over to find the gun and hat, and the tape on his right hand got caught on the door strike, the fast-closing door slamming hard on his last row of knuckles.

He could barely keep from screaming. He tucked the gun and hat between his legs and held his hand, tried to rub and shake the pain away.

A Hummer H2, an Audi R8, a Porsche Cayenne, and a Bentley all sat tidy on a white epoxy floor one level down. Flashlight helped him down the stairs and he crawled under the Porsche, knowing it would have enough clearance to let him keep his face pointing upwards.

Nose tip almost touching the chassis.

Men like the Dolphin and Coyote thought they led the dance and knew what to expect, but the Dolphin lay dead upstairs. When the god of the sun was asked about earth's tomorrow, he replied that he would only see the half of it, the moon goddess saying the same.

The police slowly closed their circle around the house, finding the body but not the gun they had expected. They searched and processed the scene, taking hundreds of photos of surfaces, interiors of closets, and the unlit fridge, going down to the garage and into the darkness. Two of the police shone flashlights through the windows of the cars and made half-squat glances beneath them. Daphnis rested the cap and gun across his chest and tried to calm the scream of his knuckles.

A rat ran out from beneath the Hummer and dissuaded the police from doing more in the dark.

"We need lights," said one over the radio.

They manually opened the garage doors from within and the breeze and light made Daphnis feel exposed.

"We need tape across here."

Chit-chat and semi-audible murmurs for an eternity.

"Someone tipped us off..."

"Used to be a cop..."

Sounds diminishing by nightfall when the doors were closed, electricity restored. Daphnis kept staring at the chassis. Cramped but too nervous to move.

Bryan and Coyote thought of him as expendable, his body worth nothing. The Dolphin's body swollen and blue upstairs. These cars were here last week, yesterday, the house and art would belong to someone else, luxury and wealth perhaps not as fleeting as the people who possessed them.

It was the first time Daphnis thought deeply about death, that the end would not be the end of the world but the end of his eyes that saw it. This hand that aches and feet that walk. This head that knows so little.

An ambulance came for the body upstairs and the scene was sealed, cameras collected. Three bullets from an antique gun and someone at the end of the phone knowing something.

He heard the cars driving away while he shivered on the concrete floor. Waited and rolled out from under the

Porsche, triggering lights on a motion sensor. He was startled and stayed still, staring at the door up the stairs until the lights went off again.

Upstairs, it felt like he was touring a bare and gigantic tomb, moonlight shining off the floor. He rested the gun and hat on the counter and used his jacket to open the Sub-Zero freezer. Went straight for the ice bin with his broken knuckles, and the bag of ice he expected was not a bag of ice.

When he left through the back door, it took him down the slope that faced the ocean.

He stopped and tucked the gun into the back of his jeans. Later he burned the hat. On the slope he turned back to look at the house. Thought of Chloe and how much more he wanted from life.

We're all just little animals staring at the moon.

With his sore hand he held the bag of diamonds up to a distant street light.

BOOK FIVE

Chloe had almost walked back to Jenna just to get another hit.

A battle between the need for drugs and the fear of that life, pushed down through the mattress and never getting up.

She stumbled and felt dizzy and got sick.

She was in a movie about a girl who collapsed by a road and a woman called an ambulance and nice hands picked her up, put her on a paper plate and they were just looking, they weren't going to eat her.

Some kind of holiday came into her veins and the movie had such a happy ending.

Under lights that were cold as snow and on another bed she didn't want to be on, the girl looked up and saw her dad, her dad's sweet face with its lines from laughing, older from crying, and even though everyone was crying, the ending was just so happy.

"I want this to be real," she said.

"It is," said Sue. "It is, my little baby."

And can the trumpets do it?

Can they do what they were made for?

A man felt love and he melted brass. He shaped it and gave it keys to register the seasons of his love and he gave it a shape that meant it would always yearn and cry out, stretch for the very thing that made it.

Can this city, likewise, tell its own true story, not the one of suffering and rivals, of neighbours screaming from windows, but the story of its architects and carpenters, who tried and failed, who brought patience and dreams to the movement of their fingers, because it is a story not of shelter, not of business, but of love?

Every lonely one of us wants, and some of us get to have, and some who have will never have enough, and the brave will try to make a record of their wanting.

And let everyone in this city now rise up and blow soft notes on a trumpet.

For Daphnis came to the hospital that night and saw the love of his life.

Pause for a moment and let the whispers breathe.

You should hear this place at night.

It is not my business to pray, but I do have rituals and incantations. I have seen monks on Mount Athos mutter Kyries to their god while they wipe their tables after a meal, and I like to copy their gestures. I turn off some of the lights at night and let my lips move—an ancient language rooted in want that was never written down. I want them to find peace. May the darkness bring you peace.

Doctors speak of stages of decline, and the people who sleep the most here are those closest to death. My turning out the lights is immaterial to them. But the others—the ones who may live here for years—are the opposite. They don't sleep, no matter how dark I make it. Their memories seem to twitch and come alive at the end of every day, the ghosts rise up, and just as I mutter my ancient language, they whisper their own. Remembering the jokes that led to first kisses and arguments with old colleagues.

You can picture us now, lights going off and coming on. I check in with the ones who can't sleep, ask if I can add to their whispers, reimagine the stories of their lives and remind them of the role I played. Dim the lights before I flick them off.

I have told this story of Daphnis and Chloe in so many different ways. It was first told to me, written in my honour, by a man named Longus at the peak of the Roman Empire. He was either watching the world ripen to its fullest, or more likely feeling sad about its decline. I can't remember. In any case he told a story about two foundlings who couldn't sleep when they were apart, nor when they were together. Young lovers who couldn't keep their hands off each other.

I try to picture what my friends here were like in their youth. Before the blindness and the strokes. Many of the men still try to wear suits. Is it indecent to think of them, their aches, their wives once girlfriends opening legs like tulips to the sun? They whisper about everything their bodies used to do.

Just last night the mute woman sat beside her blind husband's bed and watched him sleep. I came to the door to turn off their light and she got up herself and dimmed it.

She left the room and I watched her wander. Past the lounge and the nurses' station, past the rec room and my little library where the books always sit like the residents themselves—neglected except by the curious. She looked as if she was either seeking or remembering.

We walked together to the mosaic I had made. In the dim light those golden squares seemed to come alive or at least respond to the lights going on and off through the corridor and ward. It felt like we weren't just staring at the mosaic but living inside it, every doorway, lit and unlit, was a square.

The water fountain stood in the middle of the niche and she leaned forward and drank, and then she straightened and put her fingers on the tessellae.

Her face was partly paralyzed, but I could see her lips moving and I put my ear to them.

Her fingers rested on the depiction of two deer standing at the edge of a dark but comforting forest. The deer stood facing the sea.

On the west coast of that island was the most beautiful place on earth.

Lina whispered to Daphnis, "Let her be. Just be yourself."

And Daphnis and Chloe took the van and drove for hours, through fields and down a nave of trees, past a blue-collar town where people pulled curtains across their sadness.

They didn't eat. Chloe did most of the driving.

They stopped halfway across the island at a tourist attraction where the trees were eight hundred years old. There were platforms built around some of the trees so that people could climb up and get a better sense of them, measure their bodies and their children against the scale of those giants whose tops were invisible from their base.

All the people clambering and taking pictures became irritating to Chloe. She saw a tree with a sign on it saying THESE ARE BURN SCARS. Four little arrows pointing to folds in the bark where the tree had burned and healed itself, burned and healed again. She looked up and guessed there were other scars higher on the tree.

"Let's go," she said.

The van was wide and they didn't hold hands and when Daphnis drove she looked at him, at his jawline, and perhaps one moment he was thinking an angry thought and she saw the dark motive of every man, the impulse to fight and take, and she felt her own flash of anger. Come the days, her anger would arise and scream, the need to take *back* triumphant.

They pulled over at a gas station and she bought a lot of candy. Wine gums, Sour Patch, and Snickers. A feeling like the front of her body was a dam and behind it grew a tide of plastic elation and panic and she pulled over later to be sick, felt a final sweat, and the road began to open.

Worry among the parents never ended.

No talk of when they might come back, no measuring what had happened. Charlie saw Sue taking a pill in the morning and said, "Maybe you should stop."

"I'll try," said Sue. "I'm trying."

For several nights Daphnis and Chloe stayed at a trailer park, at the end of a row where their neighbour was an older woman who had never had a family. The new young couple seemed a sweet conjuring and on the second day she brought them gifts, some bread and sandwich meat and a box of wine and cups.

"No harm in a little wine," she said.

The three of them sat by a fire that night in front of the woman's trailer.

"You should go for a walk in the woods. No one comes out of that forest the same."

Those nights alone in the van were hard for them. His Chloe. His best friend. Not his or anyone's. Wanted to know what she was thinking, where she had been. Wanted to tell her how he had tried.

He didn't know how to be close to her and she didn't yet know how to reclaim her skin.

Where should she take her skin? Slouch and make a cage of her shoulders. Live alone in a high blue room or nibble lettuce at a quiet kitchen table in a landscape paralyzed by snow. Paralyzed by anger. This fucking anger has to go somewhere.

"Don't look at me," she said when she was changing in the van.

No skin, not a body, just a dripping nerve that wept when the wind blew.

Memories of the heroin were sweet and taunting and when she closed her eyes she felt fingers pushing on her, a curious doctor saying, *Here, how about here, does it hurt when I press here*.

"Everything hurts," she said.

At the fire in front of her trailer the woman told them, "You have choices. I think I had a choice. Not sure how it happened, but I guess I chose this. I'm so glad you guys turned up."

Daphnis, habitually quiet, held Chloe's limp hand while the woman talked.

"You've got your whole life ahead of you."

Later that night Daphnis filled the five-gallon water jug in the dark with the communal hose and carried it one-handed back to the van. Chloe drank wine from a plastic cup and watched him heave the jug up onto the floor of the van by the bed.

"It's heavy," he said.

"You're spilling it."

She had her back wedged against the corner, sitting on the bed surveying it all in the dark with a kind of contempt she'd never known. Dirty mattress, piles of clothes, going to the outhouse, and nowhere to cook except at the barbecue where rats and raccoons were dominant.

"Where are we?" she said.

She stood up with her wine, head bowed to avoid the ceiling. Stared at the poster of the sailboats and picked at a corner of it with her back turned to Daphnis. On their way out of town they'd passed the sidewalk outside the Salvation Army where people on tranq were bent at ninety degrees and turning into the very demons they'd been running from, a picture of hopelessness that arose behind her eyes as she stared at the poster.

"I'm not a kid."

She drank her wine as Daphnis dipped his toothbrush in the mouth of the water jug.

"I'm not a kid, I said."

"I didn't say you were."

She pulled the poster off the steel and stared at the steel and thought they'll never know. No one's ever going to see what's in her head.

"I'm gonna sell the van," she said.

"Why?"

"I hate it. I can't stand up in it. I don't want a... I don't want a fucking van with a bed in it."

"You're just tired."

"Am I?"

"I don't know."

"You don't know."

He put his hand out towards her and she drank.

"You don't know anything," she said.

"It's okay."

"You don't know me."

"I do."

"You don't." She took his wrist and put his hand on her belly. "I'm not real. I'm just a bag."

She drank the rest of her wine.

"Feel that?" she said. "I'm a bag. You just pour it in. I'll be whatever you want. Fill me up. I'm not real, so how can you know me?"

"Why are you mad?"

"Why am I mad? Where are we going? Why are we camped here?"

"I don't know."

"See? You don't know anything."

"We've got to run. We're trying to figure it out."

"Are we? What if there's nothing to figure out? What if you're alone? Because I'm not here. I'm not real. What do you do then? You're alone and there's nowhere to go and there's no future because it's all so fucking ugly. Empty."

He could feel her shaking and a sob coming.

"There's nothing to figure out," she said. "I could see those men. I never wanted to look in their eyes, but I saw them sometimes. And they're bags just like me. Nothing in their eyes, or some kind of, of dream or something, but they're not seeing me. Seeing some dream of somebody else and behind it is nothing. We're all nothing. Nobody was there on those beds." She used his hand to hit her stomach.

"Stop," he said. "It's okay."

"It's not. It's not okay. I want this bed out of here. I want to sell this. I want to get out of here. I can't breathe."

She stepped out of the sliding door and leaned forward on the grass.

Black night air and trailer after trailer of people chewing their teeth in their sleep. A propane lamp next door sounded like a man breathing on glass, forever exhaling, and it made her panic deepen.

Daphnis stepped out and put his hand on her back.

"Don't," she said. "I can't breathe."

They retreated as solitudes and Daphnis felt a wave of pain from his broken knuckles. Stared at the night and looked back at her.

"I looked for you every night," he said. "I didn't sleep. I worked for you. I knew you weren't gone. I knew we'd figure it out."

"So why didn't you find me?! Those fuckers had me right there! You fixed their cars!"

"I tried."

"You tried!"

The night turned red for her. Too many layers of incomprehension and disbelief and Daphnis suddenly seeming like a stranger, like she hated him, and even now, even as she was angry enough to stab him, she felt beneath it all a fear. Everywhere, all the time. The possibility that the apes would come out of those woods and they would keep her in the van forever.

She looked around and paced and tried to calm her anger, put her back against the van so no one could come at her, and she found a breath.

"We'll figure it out," he said.

She laughed.

"There's nothing to figure out. I know the answer. The answer to everything is nothing. There's no... We can't change anything."

She breathed again.

"I was in a black room somewhere and then I was in a different room, and the different room... it made me understand. Everything's just going to happen. I can change little things, but in the end it's... I had this thought. Today was the future of the day before. Right? The dream of the day before. And what's so fucking good about today? We dream about who we're gonna be... who we want to be, and we've got no idea. We didn't plan this. We didn't plan yesterday to be standing here under this ugly light. We just end up in different rooms. And then it ends. Everything changes. I thought someone would get me. Or wake me up. You. Or Dad. And I realized there's nothing underneath us. Underneath the ground. If there was no ground, we'd be falling."

"But there is a ground," he said. "Right here."

She looked down at herself. Held up the backs of her hands. Not a kid, a woman, shaking. It's the girls and women who give hope, is what the stories say. Who pick up babies and smile through school, tell their grumpy husbands there will be something to look forward to tonight.

"I'm empty," she said.

"You're not. We'll go somewhere. We can choose."

"You don't know anything."

That night she had a dream. Hot with bad wine, she wandered to a white Winnebago with drapes across every window.

She turned on the light above the stove and behind her were two benches with a table fixed between them.

A woman with long red hair and a white chemise, sweaty from making love, took the bench across the table from Chloe and rested her chin on the heel of her hand.

"Do you know that story where the man says *remember where you came from, remember your first love*? He told you to write it all down."

She tapped an empty notebook on the table.

"Your fingernails scare me," said Chloe.

"There's food," said the woman. "Reward for anyone who overcomes, and denied for those who don't. I can make it for you, but you have to write it down. You have to overcome."

"I can't."

She stared at Chloe and looked towards the bedroom where a bright light shone from the half-open door, so bright that Chloe couldn't look.

"The truth's in there," said the woman. "And secrets. Answer to the question of whether we're all just the one person, even the one you hate. Listen..."

Breath and moans coming from inside the light. One couple, two couples, three.

"Write it down and remember," said the woman.

"I don't want to."

"Driving is a kind of writing," she said. "I'll warrant that. People drive away to forget, but they remember. They always remember. And the story's written forever by the highways."

Breath still came from the bedroom and mimicked the sway of the truck.

"Roads are stories about people wanting to leave."

Chloe drove and tried to follow the road but the steering was soft and she felt the gravel on the shoulder.

"Where will we go?"

"I don't know," said Chloe. "I just want to drive."

In the other direction came a car lit within by the same bright light in the bedroom, too bright for Chloe to see who was driving, and soon a few more drifted past.

"I want to stay in the dark," said Chloe. "Please."

The woman reached over and turned the headlights off and neither saw anything now, the truck losing the road and the dirt making the movement rhythmic, rolling over a carpet of cats and frogs whose complaints made Chloe cry.

"I don't want to hurt them."

"People do terrible things."

Chloe pressed the brake and they stopped.

"Remember your first love. Write it down."

"I can't."

"Write down what happened to you."

Daphnis parked the van near the rainforest by the far coast, not the farthest west you could go on the island but an ending nonetheless.

Mist on his and Chloe's faces when they walked, alone like the world's first couple.

Daylight had not been allowed unmeasured in those woods for centuries and the layers of life and death were uncountable. Cedar and Douglas fir collapsed, mushrooms oozing in a bed of moist corruption, and there its opposite took root: ferns so green and trees so strong, a vital city springing from its graves.

The forest floor was so thick with old and new that it was dangerous to walk on. You could sink, or break an ankle, so boardwalks were built to guide people. The boards themselves had grown rotten in places, but they told Daphnis and Chloe where to go.

They were quiet as they walked, put on their jackets as the chill grew.

Chloe had a thought that made her sore, a memory of another couple who if alone in the woods would have kissed and laughed, the girl skipping ahead to turn and lift her shirt.

Could she be with him again?

Would he ever understand?

"I don't know what I did," she said.

"What do you mean?"

"What did I do? Why did they do that to me?"

She crossed her arms and felt sickened even by the touch of her own fingers.

Darkness in the woods, and the darkness should have scared her, the leaves always weeping and the darkness also sweet. How comforting it can be to succumb, to see the mice at the edges of our vision and find them soft, not scary. To think of herself alone in those black rooms and want that solitude. Turn to the mice and follow their number back to the cracks and voids and the places everyone else has feared and left behind.

"I'll kill them," said Daphnis.

They made their way through the forest to a beach beyond it, where the tides were famous for how quickly they came and went. Two deer emerged from the woods, farther down the beach, nosing the sand and looking up as if for news. Creatures from a story.

Chloe stared and walked.

"I'm afraid of hating everything. I'm afraid to tell you what happened," she said. "But I think I'll die if I don't."

She started crying and most of it came out in tongues, a pentecost of grief, Chloe sobbing out pictures that hung in the clouds and the mind of Daphnis, of teeth and stubble and unholy noises, of men who refused to see what was in front of them, black-and-blue sounds that never should have been heard above the underwater sinks they came from.

They sat on a rock and she talked about whatever she could remember and he held her from behind as the tide went out.

"I tried to think of you," she said. "I tried so hard not to be there."

Such a cold day.

The beach flat and dun and the sky vacated.

Daphnis wandered alone for a while with his own confusion and anger, higher up where the water seldom reached.

He looked back at her and the ocean and wrote CHLOE in the sand with a stick.

She was afraid of motels and had moments of confusion, happy one morning when she was convinced that none of it had ever happened. They checked into a place called the Wayfarer and as soon as she was in the room she started shaking, tried to push a dresser against the front door. She didn't sleep and Daphnis held her in the shower until there was no hot water. Cold, compelling clarity to the next day's light, she sat in a towel on the bed feeling like she had swallowed a knife.

They watched TV for a day, people chatting about how to be perfect, an old cop show, a quiet long shot on Court TV of a mother and father being sentenced for chaining their children to their beds. Kids growing up in a filthy house, not being fed, getting beaten by their mother and touched by their dad, and Chloe felt a strange comfort watching the still shot of the courtroom, feeling lucky she had the parents she had. The kids gave testimony about how their lives were affected, what they suffered, and what their days were like now; one of them, a girl Chloe's age in college, stood at a podium, crying and smiling at the same time. Defiant.

"I'm a fighter, I'm strong, and I'm shooting through life like a rocket," she said. "Because I know the worst is behind me."

Chloe thought about that phrase, *behind me*. Wanting to put every minute behind her, each morning and night stacked up behind her as their trip continued. Barriers to remembering. Barriers to keep them from coming through the door.

"I'll never get rid of it," said Chloe. "How will I get rid of this... I've got this horrible story inside me. How can I forget it?"

They drove farther inland and every exit became a question.

Frank had been coming to the garage before everyone else most days. Five in the morning, the fragile hour when the worried wish the sun would hurry up.

He turned on the overheads and the radio in the office, looked at the calendar on the wall, and Bryan hit his neck with the side of his hand. Frank's head struck the edge of the desk as he fell.

Coyote had got his cop friends to comb the Dolphin's house. They found more cash in the walls but no diamonds. One of them pored over crime scene photos and made comparisons to the house. Shots of the fridge and freezer revealed that a bag of ice was missing.

Coyote knew that Daphnis had been in there and got the gun. He knew he had the diamonds.

"Maybe they're like little birds or maybe they're like horses," he was saying. Standing over Frank in the paint booth of the garage. "Lots of stories about girls. Romance.

All the guys not getting enough over the years, making girls into something they're not. Little birds."

Frank woke up with his hands duct-taped to the old wooden chair from the office. His ankles taped together. Sitting in the open-ended spray paint booth while Bryan wrapped rags around the sprinkler system.

Coyote stood in front of Frank, not a biker in a suit but a demon.

"I like thinking of them as horses. Little fillies you can *break*. And the older they get... Take anyone on their backs because we broke their spirit. You know? Bryan here probably broke her forever."

Coyote leaned in and sniffed at Frank.

"I can smell rye on you," he said. "Even with all this paint. Eh? Skinful of rye."

Frank stared at his blackened ears.

"I've known so many drinkers. So many kinds. The guys who do it for the love of life. That's you, I'm guessing. Not a loser from the get-go, right, but one of the dreamers. They get older and see what's on the other side of those dreams and the drink comes to be something else, doesn't it?"

"I don't know where they are."

Bryan came over and hit the back of Frank's right hand with a pipe. The pain put something blue behind his eyes.

The sun hadn't risen yet. Charlie wouldn't be there for two hours.

Coyote looked around the paint booth. It was enclosed on three sides, one of them with a window onto the shop floor, the open end covered with a clear vinyl curtain that they sealed when they parked a car in here. Years of spray was layered on the walls and floor and the window was painted opaque.

Bryan took an armful of oily rags from the safety cabinet across the shop floor. He stuffed them in the air duct of the paint booth.

"My friend, he parked my money in those diamonds. Rough ones worth more than cut these days. Lot of money in that bag."

"I don't know where they are," said Frank. "They took her van. They didn't say anything about diamonds."

"It's not like you guys are hard to find. Your houses. Bryan knows where you live. Your wife. One day we'll have your wife over to the clubhouse, eh, Bryan? Let her loose. We throw a party for the old ladies once a year. Think she'll come? Disgusting what happens to the body, eh. The rolls and yellow teeth. When an old lady thinks she's young. How would yours do without you, do you think?"

"There's no need..."

"Just tell me where they are. Your boy killed my friend. Ex-cop. Shot him in the head."

"Bullshit."

"Is it?"

Bryan stood behind Frank and hit his other hand with the pipe.

"Please," said Frank.

"Please what?"

"Just wait. Just wait. Let me breathe."

The pain so lonely.

Frank's father came from Lesbos, his mother from Ios where Homer was said to be buried. Story was that the poet in his older years was presented with a riddle and died in sadness from not knowing how to solve it.

Frank had thought about killing himself every day for the past few years. Maybe if he had had a gun handy... Thought about moving the steering wheel just that little bit on the highway, so easy, nothing but a spider's web holding us alive most of the time. A couple of occasions back there he drank and drank, took a few, not enough, of Lina's sleeping pills.

Still woke up in the morning.

Water still coming from the taps and his feet still moving without him having to think about it.

"Is it brave?" he asked. "Bravery?"

"What's that?"

"Keeps us going." He wished he could rub his knuckles for the pain. "Keeps us waking up. You look at me, look at someone older. Do you see bravery?"

"No," said Coyote.

"I'm thinking old people are the bravest. Keep walking through this shit. There's an old lady on my street. I see her out late, every night. Walking. Like she's looking for something she lost."

"You telling stories now, Frank? Want me to sit on the floor?"

Coyote took the pipe from Bryan.

"Just wait. I'm working it out. I'll tell you where they are. Just give... let me breathe."

He looked deeply at Coyote. Thought about that bear he had encountered all those years ago. The mother. This was not that bear.

Bryan stepped out and found the tanks of oxygen and acetylene. Attached the rosebud torch and pulled on the fifty-foot hose. He lit a small flame first, letting the fire lick the mouth of the torch, staring at it like an ancient conjuring a bad idea, and he walked back towards the paint booth with the torch and its flame held upwards.

In Frank's mind Daphnis and Chloe were far away, maybe off the island. Texts or calls, even postcards would come with stories about their eyes opening to a world that Frank had never got a chance to know. How many years had he spent not finding new things so much as seeing and doing things in layers that only reminded him of doing them before?

"They're across the prairies by now."

"Where?"

"Driving. There's wheat and lakes. People who want to live."

"That's a pretty picture," said Coyote.

He stood over Frank and leaned forward, his hands on Frank's arms, his browbone bald like his head.

"I'm gonna burn down your garage. Maybe that will bring them home."

He stepped outside and pulled the vinyl curtain off its fasteners, took the torch from Bryan and gave it oxygen, the flame hissing, and he laid it on the floor as if presenting spoils.

All the years of labour and mistakes were alive in the pores of that concrete. Oil spills, gas, solvents, and paint. A flame rose quickly across the floor and Bryan and Coyote left.

A pretty flame, with pinks and greens, and I stood amidst it saying, "That woman walking your street is looking for her husband. Death is hardest for the ones left behind." Love saying that Love won't burn in the fire, I am greater than life and death.

The flames rose up the wall of the paint booth and made the sound of wind and then a gale, a sound Frank remembered from standing on a mountain once. The mountain in a photo on his desk that was now catching fire in the office. Plastic picture frames melting, the fire spreading everywhere, the sun god losing control of his horses and the earth asking upwards whether this was her reward for fruitfulness and service.

His shoes caught fire.

Charlie heard the explosion from his house.

BOOK SIX

Life became ash, snow became water, youth grew into something it never wanted to be. Transformation over time across that city.

When Jenna was a girl her mom was addicted to painkillers and Jenna drank Orange Crush instead of eating. Her parents fought in the backyard over money and Jenna tried to figure out life, like every little girl does, not imagining a career or motherhood, but wondering how to be loved. Some days she went to school and if she wasn't in a fight herself she was on the edge of one, tittering when punches connected and making sure the tough guys knew she was with them.

She was skinny.

She missed that skinny girl. Not the one who got into fights but the one who was noticed one day at the mall when she was fourteen. The love of her life came up to her uninvited and simply said, "You're pretty."

He was a rich boy, gentle, who went to the private school she'd heard about, forty acres on the other side of town. She had never stood close to a boy like that. Blond hair and a smile with no mischief, something simply good about him.

She met him after school, at his place not her own. Too worried that he would see how squalid her life was, she was dishonest with him even though he made her feel more honest than she ever had.

He wasn't the first boy she had made love with, but he was the first she cried with. And once they did make love she awoke a devotion and obsession in him where he felt simply lost unless she had her shoulder near his.

He played soccer and she watched his games, wondered what a life was like that allowed such bloodless competition, the handshakes between kids who wished each other well. He broke his ankle and she realized he was too kind and good for pain. The first, maybe the only, person she knew who wasn't prepared for some measure of it, not because he was weak but because he was so innocent.

All she wanted to do was to take his pain away.

She brought him some of her mother's pills and together they found a softness that standing creatures have always dreamt of, a bed at the end of a long journey. They couldn't believe how light life was.

"I got you a knife," he said.

He held it up: an old-looking blade with a carved bone handle.

"My dad got it in South Africa. He said it was charmed, and he gave it to my mom. They're the happiest parents of any of my friends'. You're not supposed to use it for anything—you have to hide it somewhere and it gives you luck."

She brought him more drugs and he bought her a locket, said he would put a picture of them in there when they were old, and she missed her period for a couple of months and realized she was pregnant.

By then they had turned to needles.

The journey was so fast. What space travel must be like, astronauts strapping themselves into a seat with all their troubles and memories in their heads, two of them such a small part of this world of troubles and memories, and they fly, on fire, shoot themselves up through the sky away from all that colour and noise to a weightless place and hang there.

Jenna couldn't remember how she grew through those days, but she remembered the labour and the baby's face and how it called her to do things she just wasn't ready to do.

They tried.

Fifteen years old, on their own, they tried, and if it wasn't for the drugs they might have made it.

"I could have made it," said Jenna, here, twenty years later, sitting in Bryan's car and saying she had to let Chloe go. This different Jenna, body that didn't feel like her own.

The skinny one woke up with their baby one day and the love of her life was cold and blue beside her. She had no idea what was real and she spent two decades turning tricks and getting clean, building a life because there was a fight in her. Taking needles in his honour, taking pain away, missing that innocence and ruining it for how many other girls.

"I'm so fucked-up," she said.

"This'll help," said Bryan.

"I had to let her go. We can't keep doing this."

"I'm not gonna stop," he said.

Bryan pushed the needle into her, the one that keeps you in space forever.

When Jenna was fifteen she walked downtown at night with the baby in the rain. Put him down on the sidewalk with the knife and the locket, can't remember if she said a prayer, doesn't want to think about any of it.

Bryan sat behind the wheel of his car and watched her peak, her head nod, her last wheezing breath, lips turn blue.

He drove her to the ravine and there were trees growing in the place where they had left other girls, other girls travelling in the bellies of wolves and vultures, these trees rising from their bodies, transformed.

There's a story about me, Cupid, having two arrows in my quiver. One kindles love and the other dispels it. The first is made of gold and has a sharp point, the second is blunt and made of lead.

Maybe it's that simple.

I think about all the wars and weapons. Metals pulled from the ground, melted and shaped, left on fields once the love and hate subside. The skin of the earth getting harder.

Chloe sold the van and they bought a beater, took a ferry off the island and drove through summer. The sun helped, and not feeling trapped by the city.

Gold attracts the front of the eyes and lead sits behind them.

Lead not only behind Coyote's eyes but in the sky outside his window.

Lead the colour of his ocean.

He stood with his hands in his pockets, gun strapped as always under his suit.

There are some with hate in their heart who do nothing but remember. All the injustices. Those who wronged them.

And there are others, like Coyote, who do nothing but plan.

He sent men out on the highway, looking for the red van. Got some cops to try to track them down.

Smoke from the garage had long blown away and his ears, as always, were on alert for movement behind him.

Yesterday was the Thanksgiving Ride.

Every year he gathered bikers—his gang and a few friendly rivals, local Harley owners and their girls—to ride through the streets and countryside raising money for local kids. Chili dog lunch at Bowen Park and a nighttime party at the clubhouse.

The Ride bought goodwill. Calmed things briefly between the gangs, kept things civil with the police, made the Jokers seem decent and benign. The money they raised got bicycles for kids—fifty of them that they gave to the cops to raffle in their precincts. And the kids loved seeing the bikers, the low-rider painted like a dragon and the Softail with carving knives as spokes. Tattoos and leather and costumes on these guys who apparently loved bicycles and kids.

Coyote wore his cut-off vest and colours, took the lead all day on his matte black Night Train that didn't shake at stops. Behind him were his gang, disciples, more or less idiots to a man, who felt powerful on this day and believed they were part of some charitable cause, something like magicians who knew every trick but still believed in magic. Carried away by the sounds and a sense of common cause.

A couple of Joker costumes, balaclavas, someone he didn't recognize yet in a white plastic mask.

This year Bryan rode his custom '98 Sportster with Cobra three-inch slip-on mufflers blowing a loud and sporty fuck-you to the riders behind him. He had trouble starting it later in the day and revved it higher than usual at stops to keep it running. Drawing attention to himself.

Coyote counselled a measured policy with revving when they were in the city near the kids. Show power when taking off, but when they were stopped and gathered he didn't want too much noise. The sound of Bryan's bike was pissing him off and he kept his distance.

There were around two hundred riders out, escorted by some cops on bikes and a few squad cars. Sky low and grey. Quite a few people out downtown doing their regular shopping and wandering, but this year like others there were plenty who came out just to see the bikes, some bringing lawn chairs and coolers.

The riders stopped for coffee and let the kids come near, some inviting little ones to hop on. Talk with their dads about custom chrome and upgrades, keeping things clean but giving the kids glimpses of the questions and perversities that lit the path of every lost soul. A biker dressed as Spiderman with a sidecar full of Chuckie dolls, and Henry, known by the gang as Tomcat, walking around shirtless with some kind of medieval mask and a massive belly, a figure of fun to the kids who had no idea what kind of filth he got up to in private.

They left their bikes unattended and drank their coffee and slowly rolled out again when Coyote fired up.

At the park for lunch there was more wandering and chit-chat. Coyote approached the guy in the white plastic mask and said, "Who's that?"

Duane lifted the mask and showed his coked-up face. "It's me," he said.

The chief of police made a speech about community, standing on the pergola with a megaphone. Coyote had a video of him spilling his seed at the Holiday Inn that had many times been useful.

Boyhood on the minds of many of them.

The chief shook hands with Coyote next to a bicycle with a ribbon on it. "This is a good thing we do," he said.

"Yeah, well," said Coyote. "A bike's a tool for getting where you're not."

Bryan was the last to get out on the open road. They had a tradition of taking a long ride into the mountains, a route to the north like an inverted U that landed them back at the clubhouse five hours later.

The cops peeled away an hour past the outskirts and the bikers opened up. Brief moment when most of them felt nothing if not happy.

Bryan's bike was okay at high revs but it was sputtering and he noticed the fuel gauge dropping. He was well behind the pack by the time they hit the mountains, and as he climbed the road his bike backfired and made some crows hop away briefly from the carcass of a squirrel.

He pulled over and turned off the bike. Mountain wind and a horizon of half thoughts.

Even in top shape his Harley wouldn't start sometimes when it was hot, so he waited. Listened to the wind and the tick of the cooling steel.

A long black BMW drove by and Bryan stared. Brake lights came on briefly but it continued along the road. A minute or two later it came back on the opposite side and stopped across from Bryan.

Phil Philetas, the old lawyer, put the window down and said, "Trouble?"

Bryan knew Phil from town—he'd gotten a few of the gang off traffic charges years ago.

"Just letting it cool," said Bryan. "Might need gas."

Phil pulled the car around on Bryan's side and put the passenger window down.

"Hop in. I'll take you to a gas station."

"It's far."

"The more reason if you need it."

They drove deeper into the mountains and Phil could sense Bryan admiring his car.

"Seven," said Phil.

"I know it."

"I've been buying things. Since my wife died. Can't figure it out. Bought some ten-thousand-dollar speakers. They're huge. She would have hated them."

"You're free," said Bryan.

"What do you mean?"

"Free of her." He snickered and Phil looked over at him.

Trees formed arches over parts of this road, darkening the car, and then went spare intermittently, opening views to the mountains above.

Bryan's words were in Phil's head like a bee.

Free of her.

A few minutes farther along, Phil turned down a logging road and said, "I need to pee. Prostate."

He stopped the car.

"I want to tell you something, but I need to pee. Get my cane, will you—it's in the trunk. Just wave your foot under the bumper there and it'll open. Can't pee without my cane."

He kept talking, Phil, while Bryan got out, even after Bryan closed the door.

"It's not because I'm free of her."

He held on to the steering wheel.

Bryan was glad to leave him talking.

"I've never felt less free. Stuck here without her. I'm getting rid of money, maybe that's part of it."

Bryan walked around to the trunk and waved his foot under the bumper to get the cane, and when the trunk opened he got shot three times in the face.

The shots startled Phil and he held the wheel tighter hearing the scream that came with them. "I'm just buying nice stuff," he said. "I always wanted nice things for her." He looked in the rear-view and could only see the open trunk and started crying gently.

Bryan had fallen extinguished to his side and Chloe stepped out of the trunk and stood over him, still firing the empty gun and screaming.

She waited.

A forest after the storm, memory of thunder. Rain quietly dripping and everything otherwise still.

She came around to Phil's window and saw him crying.

Put her hand on the glass.

Daphnis and Chloe had a bag of diamonds and a Mauser pistol with four bullets. When they heard the news about the garage, Daphnis looked at his still-useless hand and said, "You should practise."

She figured out how to open the chamber and saw how many bullets were left. "Take one shot," he said. They drove towards home and found a forest in the foothills. The bullet hit a pine that Chloe hadn't aimed at and they thought of ways to get up close on the day. The kickback and sound of the Mauser were in Chloe's dreams for weeks. An end or a beginning.

She had stared at the gunshot tree, like those others with the burn scars. "If there's a hole in you, I think it stays forever," she said.

"Maybe," said Daphnis.

So many nights of talking and crying. She drove away from him once, leaving him at the shitty motel they stayed at, and the horizon had never looked more empty.

"Those trees with the scars, they grew so big," she said. "Maybe you grow around the holes?"

He kissed her.

He went downtown on the day of the Thanksgiving Ride wearing a Jokers jacket and a black balaclava. He had a $^{5}/_{16}$ wrench and two old spark plugs, electrodes brown and partly rounded.

At coffee time when everyone was milling, he popped the boots off the plugs on Bryan's bike, front and rear, wrenched off the originals with his one good hand, and put the burnt plugs in their place, all in less than a minute.

When he heard Bryan's bike cough and pop he figured the plan might work.

Frank and Charlie's friends had all gathered around the tragedy and Phil believed he had less to lose than any of them.

"Easy to get old and figure the world should burn," he said. "But it shouldn't with you two in it."

Chloe spent close to an hour in the trunk. Nausea and uncertainty so familiar to her. Being trapped.

She held the strange handle of the pistol with a sweaty hand, and remembered, arms crossed over her chest, getting bounced around like luggage or a corpse. Eyes closed and waiting for the sound of the latch, the only agreed-upon signal.

She clenched her teeth and summoned.

The god of Light, of War. The god of Mud and Underdogs. Gods who have not been named because you don't yet know what to pray for. All of them joined hands with me and made Chloe burst from that trunk with cosmogenic force, screaming and pulling the trigger ten times more than needed, and she shot his temple and eyes.

And so the following day Coyote stood looking out at the ocean, not yet aware of what had happened to Bryan but sensing a change. Something behind him and above.

Since he was a teenager he had been an agent of death. Wisdom and strength are gained from looking death in the eye, but even more is won from being that eye looking outwards. To see at every turn what you can *take*. To be feared.

When he was in juvie at thirteen he bit the ear off the biggest savage among them. He had been perforated twenty times by that boy's sharpened toothbrush but he stood victorious with the body at his feet. The boy's ear in his mouth, Raymond staring back at all the others who held a demeanour he had cherished ever since—heads low, unable to look back at him, appalled by his smile. Frightened.

But after all these years of being death's helper he acknowledged on certain mornings that death didn't need his help.

I can't say that at this point in the story Coyote was afraid; but winter came and whispered at his neck.

He pondered Bryan's absence and sought new protégés. He had long given money to the Y and other shelters, knew when fresh meat was coming in. Poverty had grown and the shelters were fuller than ever, but lately the youth had seemed more prone to submit than to be warriors.

Coyote found himself flinching one night as he walked past the opening of the alley off Water Street. Someone emptying a bin of bottles into a dumpster: a common sound, but it felt to him like a hail of knives. Just for a second. Just long enough to make him wonder if he was getting the flu or something.

He kept to the clubhouse and beefed up security. Turned up the heat and sat at the bar and took comfort in hating others. He was wary of new faces but he wanted to watch the collapse of fresh humanity, new dancers, new girlfriends, throwing coke and H into the air and watching the ensuing Chernobyl of mistakes, his dipshit brothers fighting over nothing and everyone topless and sick. Tempted for the first time in decades to do a line or a shot.

Death blew in through gaps under doors. Pipes bursting. Fridges and TVs no longer working. It seemed nothing man-made, no machine, could ever last. Coyote's treadmill seized, as did his Lexus.

In the richest place on earth is a tribe who eat black mulberries, never smiling to each other without seeming to have eaten blood. And their lives are sugared and brief.

On the ocean floor black pearls are scattered, the only remnants of original Night.

Some people find themselves at the bottom, caught in the ocean's darkest place. And some of them, like Chloe, find the pearls.

Say your prayer: Let them swim, O Love. Let them rise in the name of love.

Those are the great survivors.

It snowed in early May that year, the latest snowfall on record.

Faces were lit by burn barrels under bridges, a landscape of doorless cars. A city, it seemed, of lost hope, tired of struggle and hate.

But Chloe had another dream.

The fight not lost in her eyes, she closed them and had visions.

She dreamt that she was on the far coast again with Daphnis, that they were in a canoe and paddling past a hill and they heard a great commotion.

They looked to the top of the rise, just up there beside them, and some antlers appeared. A caribou. First the one and then the others. Hundreds running behind them and coming to a stop. Nowhere farther to run.

She could smell them in her dream, the sweat on their hides, and could see so clearly their confusion. What now?

It was beautiful.

How they sniffed the air and looked across the water. How they bobbed and lowered their heads and turned to go back the way they had come. Changed their plans. Turned to each other for whatever was next.

Maybe she and Daphnis had truly seen this happen. Maybe her dream was real. So much of what she lived couldn't possibly be.

She saw that Daphnis had a back made of iron and he learned so many hidden and wonderful things. Confident and patient hands that kept the world running smoothly for the priests who thought they controlled it.

Daphnis had friends in other garages and they told him when certain cars came in. They learned from each other and let him visit, and in her dream he spent a night at one of these garages labouring on a car he had worked on before.

He knew the issues with its fuel line, how to remove the back seat and disable the locks and windows from within. And he worked on it through the night while Chloe called and said she felt herself swimming upwards, just like Daphnis himself had yearned to do, and she knew that she not only would make it out of the water but would swim up over the clouds.

Later in life, having learned how many opposites to joy are ranged across this world, she and Daphnis cherished every smile and small moment, learning that honey and sting alike must be savoured.

Their children played in the woods.

And like many dreams, this one had a demon and ended with the daylight.

The demon had black ears and he went to that garage when a pale sun rose, just warm enough to melt the recent snow.

The demon got into a car with maroon seats and Daphnis followed for not very long. A fire began inside the car and Daphnis was close enough behind to see him struggle.

The demon tried the doors, first his own and then the other, kicked at the windows, and flailed and shouted for help.

And the flame behaved as if it remembered itself, its purpose, redoubled and grew stronger, so strong and bright that Daphnis said he quickly couldn't see the demon, the fire burning for as long as the fuel would last, and Daphnis saw that the flame was the offspring of the sun and the sun seemed proud and the flame and the sun held open their arms and that was the day when winter ended, the sky a mosaic of gold.

EPILOGUE

The roads on the island of Ios were first laid by shepherds who thought their land, their flocks, might be world enough, who in the morning blew the grazing tune and prayed for a season of figs.

Daphnis and Chloe rented a motorbike and drove up towards the sky with the sea all around, the small engine fighting with the slope and winning, so loud that it made Chloe laugh. Despite the gravity and struggle they got faster as they crested and it felt like they were flying.

Down a cliff to the sea, so blue.

I watch Frank and Lina get dressed these days, how Lina, who can't speak, helps Frank get his shoes on in the morning. He can tie them, but she does it for him, and in her fingers is the same unwritten truth that the fingers of Daphnis and Chloe spoke on a beach in Greece years ago: Alone I am never enough.

Lina nods and writes down words and can't quite remember what some of them mean, and she waters the plant in the window of their room. She helps me and the other orderlies fold towels and bibs and feels proud for it.

Some of it might not look like love, this world. The relentless search for holier revisions, distaste for the past and present. Inside these windows is sadness over everything lost. Friends gone, and children. Outside are strip mines and burnt churches, mountains of useless computers.

Daphnis and Chloe visit this place on Sundays and Daphnis usually returns a few times a week. They bring one or two or all three of their kids, and the youngest, Phoebe, likes to crawl over Frank when he lies in bed and he gives her mints and candy that he buys at the tuck shop and hides beneath his pillow. His eyes look like ten-cent pieces resting in thimbles of milk.

It's often loud when everyone visits and I have never had much patience for family gatherings. You might not even find me in a corner. Chloe has stories about the kids and Lina touches Chloe's face sometimes, wants so badly to tell her something and she can never remember what.

Charlie and Sue have gained a lot of weight, but the years have been otherwise more kind to them. They come over with wine and Charlie pushes Frank out into the garden while Sue and Lina dance with other people at Happy Hour, usually women because the men are mostly broken.

"If I did it all again I'm dumb enough to do it in exactly the same way," Frank says to Charlie. "You were good to me. Do you wish you could take a look at a day all over again? Just a day?"

"I do."

Because he can't see, Frank tends to look inwards. Recounting.

The story he likes most is this: Once upon a time, they found two kids and called them Daphnis and Chloe. Not only when they were young but for the rest of their lives they learned that everything could be fixed; that things would sometimes get worse, then better.

Daphnis and Chloe had a bag of diamonds and a gun. They put the gun in a safe with a locket and a knife, a bracelet and a pair of red-soled shoes that Chloe wore on a couple of dates with Daphnis, her feet the match of a mother she never met. With the diamonds they bought a new garage and before their kids were born they took everyone, Frank and Lina, Charlie and Sue, to the island of Ios where Frank was born, where part of their story began.

One night on that holiday, Frank walked alone on feet forever sensitive from the fire. He had spent all day with the others and was out here now by the ocean, to think.

Imagine, he thought, *if I had missed all this.*

He looked up at the stars.

The galaxy was busier than he remembered. Satellites.

In the day you could stand on the hills of that island, look down at the plain white houses, and think of simpler civilizations, maybe wonder how it all went wrong.

Frank could see the flame travelling across the floor of the garage, burning his shoes and pants and the tape that bound his ankles. All he thought of was Lina and Daphnis. Somehow making it out to the parking lot in time to watch his life's work burn.

Up there.

How many messages of want and hope were those satellites helping to send?

That sky being paved with light.

All the old tires in the garage had caught fire and the smoke was black and oily. Flames pink and green from lithium and solvents. Fire that wouldn't go out for days and smoke that stained the buildings across the street.

A mess that Frank had made.

He was blind now but saw it all. Nothing had gone wrong.

It might not look like love, but it was.

And the part of the story he didn't know was that Daphnis and Chloe went into town that same day and watched a woman beating carpets on her balcony, getting her house back to normal for the off-season. They bought cheese, bread, and wine for a picnic and saw an overweight German man in tight red pants, who might have been me, taking pictures of a roadside shrine and smiling at a woman placing a flower upon it. Obnoxious Italian boys, many of them with faces like mine, harassed the streets on Vespas, and Daphnis rented a motorbike from a friendly man whose left eye drooped in a wink, like my own; indeed, if they had blurred their eyes they might have noticed that this charming face was everywhere that day.

And they rode their motorbike down a cliffside road to the sea.

"I don't think we've ever been alone," said Chloe. "Not like this."

In more fanciful traditions people say that my mother was Venus, that Venus herself was born from the froth of the sea and that whenever she wished to return to it she could walk on the waves, and with the touch of her rosy feet the water would suddenly calm. The sea was so still that day that kingfishers nested on the surface.

I walked some distance away, thinking of my own life, my one true love who comes to me throughout my constant journey. The day we met, eyes across the room, the first touch of your fingers. How I can never wait to see you in the morning.

I stood, unnoticed, behind a rise, along a path a goatherd once trod singing plaintive hymns to beauties he knew were beyond the horizon. That beach where Daphnis and Chloe undressed, the very site of a thousand launches and returns.

Day spilling diamonds and a fisherman pulling a line far out in the deep.

I watched all afternoon.

They stood naked in the water and came back to their towels on the sand. Chloe told Daphnis that she could see the ocean in his eyes and Daphnis tried to tell her with a kiss that he didn't care where he was, could find himself in the lowest place on earth, but with her it would always be heaven.

I saw you on that beach.

How everything blushed.

Sun coming down like a winepress on the sea.

ACKNOWLEDGEMENTS

Thank you to Bill Clegg; greater thanks to Dan Wells; and to Longus for your offering. I like to think, Suzanne, that you were a candle to him like you were to me, up there with a drink through that dark winter.

Colin McAdam is an internationally acclaimed novelist. He lives in Quebec.